HARLEQUIN

Desire

ONE HEIR...
OR TWO?

BILLIONAIRES AND BABIES

YVONNE LINDSAY

USA TODAY BESTSELLING AUTHOR

Kayla stopped the moment her eyes lit on him.

"Good to see you again, Van," she said in that husky, *come to bed* voice of hers.

No, she hadn't changed. Still with the flip attitude.

"I take it you're the one upsetting my receptionist?"

He saw the surprised hurt reflected in her clear blue gaze and wished he'd thought before speaking.

But that was how it always was with Kayla. She brought out the worst in him.

"I'm sorry," he said. "What can I do for you?"

A rapid pulse beat at the base of her throat, and he remembered just how silky soft her skin had been beneath his tongue, remembered just how she'd tasted. Desire heated his blood but he resisted, hard.

"Kayla, why are you here?"

She drew in a deep breath. "Like I said, I need your help."

"And a phone call wouldn't do?"

His secretary arrived in the doorway looking totally nonplussed, and no wonder, because she had a baby in her arms. A baby?

Van looked to Kayla. "Yours, I presume?"

And then the baby looked up and he was struck by the eyes that caught his.

"Yours, too, to be precise," Kayla said softly.

* * *

One Heir...or Two? is part of
Harlequin Desire's #1 bestselling series,
Billionaires and Babies: Powerful men...wrapped
around their babies' little fingers.

Dear Reader,

It's sometimes a very complicated world that we live in these days, but with some of those complications come choices and options that people could only dream of years ago. One of these is the storing of frozen embryos to give people a chance to have a family after medical procedures that remove that prospect from them. And then there are the moral dilemmas that arise regarding the treatment of those embryos when things change dramatically in their parents' lives.

One Heir...or Two? gives a twist to such a dramatic change when Kayla Porter is determined to fulfill her late sister's dying wish—to be a mom—but when the babies' donor dad uses all his power and money to stop her, what can she do? Can she teach Donovan Murphy to overcome the demons of his past, or will he succeed in destroying her dreams for the future forever?

I love to hear from readers. Please visit me via my website, www.yvonnelindsay.com, or pop in and chat on my Facebook page at www.Facebook.com/yvonnelindsayauthor.

Happy reading!

Yvonne Lindsay

YVONNE LINDSAY

———

ONE HEIR...OR TWO?

Recycling programs
for this product may
not exist in your area.

ISBN-13: 978-0-373-73493-1

One Heir...or Two?

Copyright © 2016 by Dolce Vita Trust

For questions and comments about the quality of this book, please contact us at CustomerService@Harlequin.com.

Printed in U.S.A.

www.Harlequin.com

A typical Piscean, *USA TODAY* bestselling author **Yvonne Lindsay** has always preferred her imagination to the real world. Married to her blind-date hero and with two adult children, she spends her days crafting the stories of her heart, and in her spare time she can be found with her nose in a book reliving the power of love, or knitting socks and daydreaming. Contact her via her website, yvonnelindsay.com.

Books by Yvonne Lindsay

Harlequin Desire

The Wife He Couldn't Forget
Lone Star Holiday Proposal
One Heir...or Two?

Wed at Any Price

Honor-Bound Groom
Stand-In Bride's Seduction
For the Sake of the Secret Child

The Master Vintners

The Wayward Son
A Forbidden Affair
One Secret Night
The High Price of Secrets
Wanting What She Can't Have
The Wedding Bargain

Courtesan Brides

Arranged Marriage, Bedroom Secrets
Contract Wedding, Expectant Bride

Visit her Author Profile page at Harlequin.com, or yvonnelindsay.com, for more titles.

To my amazing fellow Writers in the Wild,
this book is dedicated to you with grateful thanks
for all your support and companionship on
our magical Tuesday mornings.

One

Van slipped the ring into his breast pocket and snapped the lid closed on the jeweler's box in his hand. The very large near-flawless white diamond was precisely what Dani would expect when he asked her to marry him at lunch today.

He knew that wasn't all she was expecting. He cast an eye over the merger documents on his desk. The amalgamation of Dani's family business, Matthews Electronics, and his DM Security would be a match made in corporate heaven. It only made sense to carry their relationship from the boardroom into the bedroom. They were kindred spirits—both focused on their business targets, both leading professional, uncluttered lives and neither of them wanting the burden of parenthood. Neither of them expected—or particularly wanted—passionate love and romance. But they'd share respect, attraction and compatible interests—and what more could he want than that? Yep, life was pretty much perfect for the boy who grew up never feeling like he belonged anywhere, and this ring would help seal the deal.

A subtle ping on his computer screen alerted him to a message from Reception. Using his Bluetooth earpiece, he connected to Anita—his dragon at the gate, as the rest of the staff called her.

"There's a woman here to see you, Mr. Murphy. She doesn't have an appointment but she is most insistent."

He could hear the disapproval in every syllable of Anita's perfect diction. Despite himself, Van felt a smile tug at his lips.

"Does the woman have a name?" he prompted. Clearly his receptionist was flustered, a reaction infrequent enough to amuse him. It was unlike her not to give him her usual shorthand summary of details that he needed to make a decision about any unexpected visitor.

"She says she's an old friend and doesn't need an appointment."

A prickle of foreboding made the hairs on the back of Van's neck stand up. That sensation had kept him alive more than once doing his tours of duty and since, in the private sector, and he wasn't about to ignore it now.

"Get her contact details and tell her to make an appointment to come back. Thank you, Anita."

A lot could be learned from a name and contact details, especially by a man with his resources. Just before he clicked off the call, he heard a slight commotion in the background.

"No," he heard Anita say very firmly. "I most definitely will not hold—"

Then all he heard was a scuffling sound. He frowned. What on earth was going on? He didn't have to wait long to find out. The commotion he'd heard in his earpiece was very definitely coming toward him down the corridor. Van gritted his teeth in frustration. His was a specialized international security company. How secure was it really if someone could walk in off the street and cause this much of a ruckus? He was up and moving from his chair before he even completed the thought, but before he could reach the door to his office, it swung open and a woman swept in. In that split second, every notion, even the breath in his lungs, stalled right where it was.

Kayla Porter.

Damn.

The last time he'd seen her, five years ago, she'd been curled up asleep on the sofa bed of the substandard apartment she'd shared with her late sister. The bed they'd shared for a few intense, incredibly hot hours before he'd pulled himself away.

Kayla stopped in her tracks the moment her eyes lit on him. Five years since he'd last seen her and she hadn't changed a bit. Still dressed like an escapee hippie from the sixties and still with the long flowing blond hair. He could even remember the scent of the shampoo she'd used back then. Something herbal and sweet and essentially Kayla. The memory was visceral and hit him hard.

"Good to see you again, Van," she said in that husky "come to bed" voice of hers as she took a few steps into his office.

Her eyes flicked over him, from the top of his head and his precisely mussed, expensive haircut to the tips of his highly polished handmade shoes. She smiled.

"I see you can take the man out of the army but you can't quite take the army out of the man, right?" she commented with a nod to his gleaming footwear.

No, she hadn't changed. Still with the flip attitude. Still thinking she was welcome wherever she went and that people would pretty much forgive her anything.

"I take it you're the one upsetting my receptionist? You couldn't have made an appointment?"

The second the words were out of his mouth and he saw the surprised hurt reflected in her clear blue gaze, he wished he'd thought before speaking. But that was how it always was with Kayla. She brought out the worst in him. Always had, even when they were kids growing up next door to one another. Granted, she was four years younger than Van and her sister, Sienna, and her nuisance factor had correlated with the age difference. But it hadn't gotten any easier to deal with her once they'd grown up. Somehow, she always put him on edge, made him feel out of control. And that was why, after their one-night stand, he'd walked away and never looked back. Even though it made him ashamed of himself whenever he thought of it—or remembered how before Sienna had died, he'd promised her he'd always look out for Kayla.

The past always had a habit of biting you in the ass.

"I'm sorry—" he started again, moving toward her. "You're here now. What can I do for you?"

He tried not to look too closely at where a rapid pulse beat at the base of her throat, because if he did, he'd remember just how silky soft her skin had been beneath his tongue, remember just how she'd tasted. A flush of desire heated his blood but he pushed back, hard. He wasn't that man anymore. Not driven by emotional and physical need. No, he'd finally learned to control himself and his behavior. Learned not to act on impulse. Learned to weigh and consider and recognize when a situation was just risky or out-and-out dangerous. And for some reason his senses were screaming red alert right now.

Another sound from the corridor outside filtered into his office. A sound that made Kayla turn, a look of dismay on her face.

She moved toward him, her hands outstretched. "Van, I need to talk to you about something important. I really need your help. I—"

Anita arrived in the doorway looking totally nonplussed, and no wonder, because she had a baby in her arms. A baby? Van looked from his flustered receptionist to the strand of pearls clutched in a chubby fist and thrust in a gummy drooling mouth, and then to Kayla again.

"Yours, I presume?" he asked.

And then the baby looked up from her prize and he was struck instantly by the eyes that caught his. Eyes that were identical to the ones that reflected back at him every morning in the mirror.

"Yours, too, to be precise," Kayla said, softly, finding her voice again.

Kayla could see Van's mind casting back to that one night they'd shared after Sienna's funeral, gauging the age of the baby, doing the math and coming up with numbers that made no sense at all. The baby began to fret and she moved forward to take her from her very reluctant minder. If Kayla's sitter hadn't fallen through...well, if her sitter hadn't up and left her with no notice, her baby girl wouldn't be here at all.

"Come on, Sienna. We'll have none of that. Let the nice lady's necklace go."

"Sienna?"

Van's attention, locked for the past minute on the baby, now transferred to her.

"She's named for her mother. Appropriate, don't you think?"

Van gave her another hard look, leaving her in no doubt she was in for a grilling. He'd never actually said what he'd done in the Special Forces but she had no doubt that interrogation had probably been on an extensive list of lethal skills.

"Her mother? Sienna?"

Kayla turned to the receptionist, who still hovered in the doorway. "Thank you, I think we'll be fine now."

The woman looked from Kayla to Van and back again. Van seemed to come to attention.

"Yes, thank you, Anita. Could you please call Dani and tell her I'll be delayed for lunch today. Perhaps we can reschedule for dinner instead."

"Yes, sir, right away. Are you sure about…?" Anita gestured vaguely toward Kayla and the baby.

"I think I can handle them," he said firmly.

His eyes remained locked on Kayla's—silently demanding an explanation. At his words, Kayla couldn't help but feel a tingle run down her spine. Part anticipation, part fear, part sensual memory. But Van had made it perfectly clear when he'd left her without a note or a word since that he was very definitely not interested in her. She shored up her defenses and clutched Sienna to her a little more tightly, earning a surprised squawk from her little girl. Again, she wished she hadn't had to bring her precious child into this meeting. If she'd had any other choice, she'd have taken it.

As soon as the door closed, Van spoke.

"Kayla, why are you here?"

She drew in a deep breath. "Like I said, I need your help."

"And a phone call wouldn't do?"

It stung to hear him sound so dismissive, but it served to strengthen her resolve. "No, it wouldn't. Last time we saw each other—" Her mouth dried and she swallowed to moisten it. She began again, more resolutely this time. "After Sienna's funeral, you said to call you if I needed anything."

"And I meant it. But, Kayla, even you have to realize that you can't just waltz into my place of business and expect to see me straightaway."

"I'm sorry, but it's really important—otherwise I wouldn't have…"

Darn, she should just come right out with it. She looked up at him and saw a stranger. Gone was the boy next door—the one who'd received more beatings from his father than he'd ever earned, the one who'd allowed her sister to befriend him and bring him into their home, the one who as a teenager had gotten her out of more scrapes than she could remember. Gone was the soldier, gone was the passionate lover who had rocked her entire world. In his place stood a cold, controlled and distant individual. A man so unfamiliar to her now that she began to wonder if she'd ever really known him at all.

"Is it to do with her?" He gestured toward the baby.

"In a way, yes. Do you want to hold her?"

Without waiting for an answer, Kayla crossed the short distance between them and held Sienna out to her father. It should have been a beautiful moment but Van looked alternately horrified and annoyed as he instinctively put his hands out to receive his daughter.

"There, see? She's not that bad, is she?"

For a second Sienna seemed as though she'd cry and looked back at Kayla, her lip starting to wobble. Kayla forced herself to smile at her baby girl and make an encouraging sound. It seemed to work because Sienna turned her attention back to the man holding her—one dimpled little hand gripping the lapel of his suit jacket, the other reaching up for his mouth. Kayla stifled a giggle at the look on Van's face. You'd have thought she just handed him a live grenade.

There was a knock at the door to his office and an exquisitely groomed woman walked in without waiting for Van's response.

"Sorry to bother you, Donovan, but I was already in the parking garage downstairs when Anita called, so I thought—"

She stopped dead in her tracks as she looked at first Kayla, then Van holding a baby.

"I see you're busy. I'm so sorry. I'll come back later."

"No, Dani, wait. Please."

Van thrust the baby back to Kayla, eliciting a howl of disapproval from Sienna. "Don't say anything," he growled quietly at Kayla before moving to the other woman's side.

Kayla rolled her eyes at him, then faced the new arrival and, juggling Sienna on one hip, put out her free hand. "Hello," she said. "I'm Kayla. My sister and I grew up with Van."

The woman moved to accept Kayla's proffered hand. "Dani Matthews," she said smoothly but not without directing a speaking look Van's way.

The look Van shot Kayla could have cut through steel.

"If you'll excuse us a moment," Van said to Dani, waiting for her nod of acceptance.

Polished and unflappable, she inclined her head in the most fluid of actions, the movement making the perfectly blunt-edged cut of her hair swoosh forward a moment before reassuming its almost regimental perfection with not a strand out of place. Kayla found herself fascinated by it. How was that even possible with the humidity of a regular San Francisco fog? Her own hair was a perpetual tousle of long blond waves no matter what she did with it.

"Thank you," he murmured. "I'll be back shortly."

"Take your time," she replied with a charming curve of her lips, but Kayla could see her eyes remained full of questions.

Without wasting another second, Van took Kayla by her upper arm and steered her out of his office and toward Reception. She made a sound of protest but he ignored it until he'd shown her into a small conference room and the door behind them was closed.

"No more beating around the bush, Kayla. I want answers from you and they had better be good."

"Van, I wasn't kidding around. I really need your help."

Sienna whimpered a little and Kayla smoothed her hand over the baby's head nervously. Suddenly this didn't seem like a good idea after all. But she'd thought and thought and she hadn't been able to come up with any other way she could raise the money she needed.

"What's wrong with her?" Van demanded, the roughness of his voice making Sienna's whimper grow louder.

"She's hungry, and in a strange place. This is messing with her routine. I'm sorry. The timing of this is all out of whack, isn't it? I should have thought this out a bit better."

Even now her breasts tingled with that full heavy warning that accompanied nursing.

"You think? But when has that ever stopped you?" he muttered.

She ignored his question. "Five years ago you offered to be there when I needed someone. Did you mean what you said?"

She had to hope that his offer still held. Without it, she had nothing and no one and her plans for the future, her promise to her sister, would all be shattered.

Van flashed a glance at his wristwatch. A Breitling with more whizzes and bangs on it than her food processor, she noted, unimpressed. But his action was a reminder for her, as well. Time was fleeting.

He flung her another look of irritation. "I don't say anything I don't mean. How about you explain it to me. You've got ten minutes, max."

"Thank you."

She moved forward and put her hand on his chest. Even through his suit she could feel the heat that poured from his body, feel the muscled perfection of his chest beneath the expertly tailored fabric. Against her will, her body began to react—her heart rate kicking up a beat, her senses that much more focused. He stared down at her hand and then back at her. She felt a rush of color stain her cheeks and let her hand drop.

* * *

Kayla's innate ability to push his buttons hadn't lessened with the time and distance between them. He reined in his impatience and directed her to sit down. The baby fussed again, tugging at Kayla's top. Mesmerized, he watched as Kayla lifted her blouse and did something with her bra, exposing one breast and guiding her nipple to the baby's mouth. It wasn't the first time he'd seen a woman breast-feeding and it probably wouldn't be the last, but he couldn't help the fascination that poured through him at the sight.

His child—the child he'd never believed would be born—being nurtured, here, right in front of him. Her birth shouldn't have happened, not with her biological mother dead these five years. But that was one puzzle he didn't need her to piece together for him. He remembered agreeing to be a donor for Sienna so that she could have embryos stored before starting cancer treatment. The logistics of how this little girl could be his baby and Sienna's were perfectly clear. What he didn't know was why—why had Kayla carried his child?

"Explain," he said curtly, trying to fight the sensation of awe that threatened to overwhelm him.

He hadn't wanted to be a father—he'd immediately signed his paternity rights away. And that had been before he'd found out the truth about his own birthright. Before he'd learned that the alcoholism that had plagued his birth parents' lives and seen him removed from their custody as a toddler could, in part at least, be hereditary. Before he'd realized he had been heading down the same path and made a decision that he would never pass that potential legacy on, ever.

"I need money. A loan."

"That explains why you're here now but doesn't explain *her*." He pointed at the baby. "Sienna and I had an agreement. If she couldn't go through with embryo transfer, they'd be donated to research or—"

Destroyed. Even he couldn't bring himself to say the word out loud. At the time it hadn't meant all that much to him. But now, faced with living proof? It was another thing entirely.

Kayla filled the silence. "Before she died, she changed her mind. With her lawyer's help, she amended the paperwork and donated the embryos to me so that the children she'd always wanted would still have a chance. I promised her that her dream would still come true."

"And now you want money from me for maintenance, is that it? For a child I don't want?"

The words hung baldly in the air between them. He'd been deliberately provocative with his phrasing and could see Kayla fighting back her instinctive response to snap back—they'd frequently rubbed each other the wrong way in the past and today was a perfect example of that. When she'd composed herself, she spoke.

"Not for maintenance for Sienna, no. You may find it hard to believe, but I didn't enter into parenthood lightly. I saved hard, I have a job I love and she has had excellent care while I work. But things have changed and I wouldn't be asking you for help if it wasn't vitally important. We've..." She seemed to choose her next words very carefully. "We've suffered a bit of a setback and I just need a loan, until we're back on our feet."

"A loan?" He searched her face to see if she was lying. "How much?"

He reached in a pocket for his cell phone, flicked out the stylus, opened a blank memo and put the device on the table next to her. "Here, put your account details in there and I'll get my bank to transfer the money directly to your account."

When Kayla didn't move to pick up the stylus, he paused.

"What is it?" he asked.

"Just like that?"

"Like what?"

"Any sum I mention. You'll just give it to me?"

That sense of foreboding washed through him again. "What's this about, Kayla?"

She adjusted the baby in her arms, and when she looked back up at him, he could see her eyes shimmer with tears.

"I miss her. Don't you?" she whispered.

Van felt his gut twist in a knot. Yes, he missed her sister—she'd been his best friend growing up, after all, and it hurt to think of a world without her in it— but in many ways she was a reminder of his failures, of a past he was none too proud of. After she died, and particularly after that night with Kayla, he'd resolved to never look back, to only look forward.

"Yeah, I do," he acknowledged. "But we have to move on, right?"

She nodded. "That's what I'm doing. I'm moving on. I've made plans, very specific plans."

Van's spider senses were screaming. "Tell me," he intoned cautiously.

"I'm going to have the rest of your babies, Sienna's remaining two embryos. I was on track. I was going to space each of the pregnancies two years apart but—"

Whatever she said next was lost in the buzzing sound in his ears. *Babies?* Everything in him protested. Kayla's voice finally penetrated the fog.

"—and with the clinic closing down, I can't wait until I've built up my savings account to support two more individual pregnancies. Time is running out."

A shudder of horror rippled through him. This couldn't be happening. Not now that he knew about the awful heritage that had been passed down through generations on both sides of his family. And certainly not now that he was on the verge of expanding DM Security and merging not only with Dani Matthews's company but with the woman herself.

Suddenly the diamond solitaire ring he had in his breast pocket felt like it was burning through the lining of his suit. He and Dani were totally on the same page on this subject. They gave to the community through their philanthropy and their skills. They had no desire to add to the world by having children. In fact, it was something they both specifically planned to avoid. Bad enough that Kayla already had one baby with his DNA. One child with a genetic predisposition for alcoholism was more than enough. But more? Being raised by a mother as flighty and unreliable as Kayla? It was a recipe for disaster.

"No," he said emphatically.

A small frown pulled between Kayla's brows. "No, you're not going to loan me the money?"

"No, you're not going to have those babies."

Two

"I beg your pardon?"

"It's not going to happen. Not again."

Kayla began to protest. She couldn't believe her ears. "Five years ago, you said—"

He cut her off. "I will fight you on this with every last cent I have if necessary. I made a mistake agreeing to Sienna's request to serve as her donor in the first place. I'm not compounding that mistake by assisting you now."

"Well, that's where you're wrong. I'm the one who makes the decisions about what happens with the embryos, not you."

"Not once my legal team gets a hold of this. I can keep this tied up through the courts for as long as it takes, and I will."

Who was this man? She barely recognized him. But once upon a time he'd been different. He'd wanted to help. Maybe she could still reach that man somehow. She had to try. For her sister's sake.

"We both loved her, Van. Don't you remember why you wanted to help her in the first place? Because you supported her and wanted her to fulfill her dreams. That's exactly what I'm trying to do here. See her dreams come to fruition."

"Don't, Kayla!" He spoke sharply and baby Sienna, startled, popped off her breast.

Kayla quickly covered herself up again. "Don't what, Van?"

"Don't try to use Sienna to manipulate me. Everything is different now. Sienna's dead. Her dream of motherhood died with her," he said bluntly.

Kayla rose to her feet and rested Sienna against her shoulder, rubbing her little back more for her own comfort than for the child's.

"No, Van, they didn't. This beautiful little girl is proof of that. And I'm going to see to it that she doesn't grow up without a brother or a sister. You, more than anyone, should understand why I'm determined to do that."

"Be prepared for a long fight, then, because there is no way I'm sanctioning the birth of any more of my children. Not now. Not ever."

Kayla forced a smile to her lips. "It doesn't really matter whether you sanction them or not. You have no say. You signed your paternal rights away, remember?"

"Nothing is ever carved completely in stone,

Kayla. And I have more than enough money to ensure that you won't be permitted to go ahead with this."

"We'll see about that," she answered with an equally determined tone. "You know, I feel sorry for you. You've become cold and unfeeling. Somewhere in the last five years you lost your heart."

Kayla could barely think straight on the drive home. Some of it she put down to hormones. After all, she'd already begun the preparation for the embryo transfer as soon as she got the letter from the clinic to say they were closing. But now she had to decide if she was going to go through with it. And she had to decide whether to go with the single transfer, like she'd done with Sienna, and hope for the best or take the option of a multiple transfer of both remaining embryos with its higher likelihood of a multiple pregnancy. If only she wasn't on such a short time frame. She'd budgeted so carefully to ensure she could have her sister's children without putting herself in dire financial straits. It wasn't cheap raising a kid, but with lots of overtime, diligent planning and a strict savings plan, she'd tucked away a tidy nest egg. But would it stretch to cover a multiple birth? No matter which way she looked at it, she'd be coming up short somewhere.

Well, she told herself optimistically, it wasn't as if she couldn't keep working and continuing to build her nest egg for now—even if the cost of day care for Sienna would now eat into her earnings. She wondered why her housemate, Zoe, had just up and left her like that. No notice, no anything. It was just weird. She and Kayla had enjoyed what Kayla thought was a fair arrangement—in exchange for an allowance, room and board, Zoe cared for Sienna while Kayla was at work. Zoe had never once mentioned she was unhappy with their situation.

Mind you, compared to living on the street, as Zoe had been when Kayla met her—down on her luck and down to her last five dollars—staying with Kayla must have been a massive relief. In fact, it was Zoe, an out-of-work child-care provider, who'd suggested she look after Sienna in the first place. So why had she just up and left?

By the time Kayla reached the two-bedroom apartment she rented on the outskirts of Lakeshore, she was no closer to finding an answer. She let herself inside and put Sienna, who'd fallen asleep in the car, into her crib. Kayla paused and gazed lovingly at the little girl. The daughter of her heart, but very much Sienna and Van's child at the same time.

Why had Van been so distant, so determined that no more of his and Sienna's children be born? It didn't make sense. He'd willingly entered into the arrangement with her sister.

Well, whatever, she would still go ahead. She'd made a vow and she wasn't going to break it. It would take a lot of planning, a lot of organization—two things that had never been her strong suits. But she'd built those skills over time. She'd needed to, in order to prepare herself for becoming a single mother. The important thing, she knew, was to take things one step at a time. So for now, her first major headache would be getting the baby back into the day care where she'd been before Zoe had moved in.

Kayla reached for her phone and noticed she had a message waiting. She frowned slightly, wondering why she hadn't heard the phone ring before realizing the sound had been turned off. Strange, she didn't remember doing that. She started to listen to the message, hoping that maybe it was from Zoe, with an explanation about where the heck she'd taken off to today.

But no, it wasn't from Zoe—it was an automated message from her bank, notifying her that her account had gone into overdraft. That couldn't be right—in fact, it had to be downright impossible. Nausea rose in Kayla's gut as she pulled up her online banking app on her phone and checked her balance. But there it was on the screen, plain to see. The entire balance of her account had transferred out last night. But how...?

With shaking fingers, she keyed in the phone number for the bank and went through the menu options that would finally lead her to a human voice. Kayla felt her throat choke as she told the customer service rep just how much money should be in her account. She ought to know. After all, she checked it on her phone every night. And last night... The sick dread that enveloped her thickened and made her stomach flip uncomfortably. Last night she'd been checking her balance when there'd been a knock at the door to her apartment. She'd left her phone on the coffee table when she'd gone to answer and Zoe had been alone

in the living room for about five minutes. Through
the roaring sound in her ears, she could just hear the
customer service rep.

"You made a large withdrawal last night, Ms. Porter.
It's all there on the screen—a payment to one of your
regular payees, a Ms. Zoe Thompson."

"But I didn't do it. She must have done it herself."

Kayla swallowed back the tears that collected in
her throat. All her money. Gone. How the heck was
she going to cope?

"Did you give Ms. Thompson access to your account? Under the terms and conditions—"

"I'm well aware of the terms and conditions, and
no, I didn't give her permission to access my account."

"Ms. Porter, even if the payment was made by mistake, please be advised that we cannot reverse that
payment without the consent of the person who owns
the account the funds were paid into."

"But I didn't authorize the payment!"

Kayla's voice rose on a desperate note and in the
bedroom she heard Sienna stir—the sound of her
mother's distress obviously having woken her.

"Ma'am, if we assist you to recover a payment
made from your authorized mobile device, we will
have to charge you an electronic credit recovery fee.
You'll find the fees set out in our guide."

"Whatever, do whatever you can, whatever your
fees are. I accept. I need my money back."

It was only later, when the bank called her back
to say that Zoe had closed out her accounts and the
funds could not be retrieved, that Kayla felt all hope

die. After filing a claim with the bank and reporting the theft to the police, Kayla finally gave in to the tears that had burned at the back of her throat for what felt like hours.

Kayla looked around her. Her only remaining belongings were her furniture, her personal things and the small amount of cash in her purse. Zoe had left her with nothing else. No backup money, no nest egg. Zip. Zero. Nada. Rage, fear, confusion and a deep sense of violation all jangled within her. When she'd brought Zoe into her apartment, adamant in her belief that giving another person a fair chance to make a good life would help put something worthwhile back into the universe, she'd thought she was making a positive difference in the other woman's life. And she'd trusted her. So much so that she'd left Sienna with her on a day-to-day basis.

She knew Zoe had had a hard past, having to look out for herself after losing her job and being thrown out of her apartment by her boyfriend. Kayla knew Zoe didn't trust easily, but she'd believed they'd gotten past that and thought Zoe had learned to see the good things that life had to offer. And Zoe had at that, a scathing little voice inside Kayla said. She'd seen what Kayla had to offer and she'd taken it—all of it.

Kayla brushed tears from her cheeks. It was all her fault. She trusted people. Always. Now it had bitten her well and truly in the backside. The hard reality of what this meant pressed down on her like a ton of lead.

"Think, Kayla, think. And breathe. You can't lose it now," she said firmly to herself, desperately trying to calm the shudders that now began to ripple through her body.

She tried to center herself—to breathe in slow and deep and find the inner calm that was usually never far from the surface of her mind—but all to no avail. The police hadn't been optimistic about her chances of getting her money back. Despite the information she'd given them about Zoe, she was just one opportunistic thief in a great big city full of them. She could even have gone out of state by now.

What the heck was she going to do? Her mind remained a blank. It was hopeless. She was hopeless. She needed money—those precious savings had been for her babies' future and to help her raise them, not to mention covering rent and utilities while she couldn't work—but who would loan her what she needed? The bank clearly wouldn't be any help, since they seemed to hold her responsible for losing the money in her account. She didn't have any family left. Most of her friends were in the same financial situation as she had been before she'd decided to have Sienna's kids—choosing to live in the present rather than plan for the future. So, if her friends were out, who did that leave?

One name whispered through her mind, making her nerves vibrate with tension and a swarm of butterflies skitter about in her stomach—Van Murphy. Even though he'd made his position painfully clear today, perhaps with time he'd soften his stance. Surely any man with a shred of decency left in him would want to help his children? It wasn't as if he was strapped for cash.

But no, she remembered the coldness on his face

as he'd threatened to keep her from using Sienna's remaining embryos. He wouldn't help her. In fact, he'd do whatever he could to stop her.

There was no way she could afford a legal battle—especially against the kind of lawyers he could afford. She'd have to scrape together whatever resources remained and go through the procedure without any kind of nest egg.

The alternative was giving up on those babies and her promise to her sister completely—and that was something she would never do.

Van ended the call with his lawyer and calmly and deliberately slid his cell phone back into his pocket. He didn't dare move, or he might destroy something, although right now a bar brawl would come in handy to help him relieve the anger that infused every cell in his body.

She'd gone and done it.

Despite what he'd said, or maybe in spite of it, she'd carried on with the transfer of Sienna's remaining embryos before he could arrange an injunction to stop her. Two embryos, to be precise, if his lawyer's information was correct. Van slowly let go of the breath he'd been holding and focused on the picture on the wall of his office. Normally the vista, painted from the balcony of his home overlooking the sea on the Monterey Peninsula, calmed him. Reminded him of just how far he'd come. But nothing calmed him now.

This was his worst nightmare come to life.

For the first time in a long time, he was lost for what to do. Automatically he pulled out his car keys. He shrugged into his suit jacket and walked down the corridor and into his private elevator. Down in the parking garage, he slid onto the fine dove-gray leather seat of his late-model Audi and activated the GPS—inputting the address he'd committed to memory about two hours after Kayla had left his office just over a month ago.

He hadn't wanted to see her again—hadn't wanted to need to have this conversation—but with her decision to ignore his wishes, he had no other option. Anger rolled in waves beneath the surface, forcing him to utilize every last ounce of training he'd ever endured to keep it under control. One step at a time, he reminded himself. His primary objective right now was to see her, talk to her. What he wanted to say— well, he had no idea yet, nothing civil, anyway, but he knew something would come to him.

The roads were relatively quiet heading out of the city and he made the journey to Lakeshore in good time. Van's brows pulled into a frown when he saw the red-and-blue flashing lights as he drove up to Kayla's apartment building. He got out of his car and locked the doors.

He scanned the numbers on the rows of apartments and his frown deepened as he saw that Kayla's was very near where two police cars jutted out from the curb, along with an ambulance. Even from where he was, Van could hear the angry yelling of a woman the cops were guiding toward one of the cruisers.

"You owe me, Kayla! You owe me! You were supposed to help."

Van's blood ran cold. Had this crazy woman attacked Kayla? He quickened his step and drew closer to the crowd that had gathered on the sidewalk. Two police officers tried to restrain the wild-eyed woman, who spat and bucked and twisted and fought them with every step. Where the hell was Kayla in all this? Van looked up to a second-story balcony where a curtain billowed out through a broken glass slider. Without realizing he'd made a decision, he pushed his way through the crowd and started toward the building, only to be stopped by another officer on the sidewalk.

"Sir, you can't go up there."

Like hell he couldn't. "Kayla Porter, where is she?"

"And you are?" The officer gave him a hard stare.

"A friend. A *family* friend," he emphasized.

"She's over there in the ambulance, sir, with the baby."

Ambulance? A cold rush of fear washed through him. Was she hurt? Was the baby hurt? Without another word to the officer, he strode toward the ambulance. As he neared the back of the vehicle, he spied Kayla inside, a stark white dressing on her forehead. His gut knotted until he saw the sleeping baby in her arms—not crying, not visibly injured, he noted almost immediately. He felt his taut muscles begin to ease. They were okay. A ridiculous sense of relief coursed through him, replacing the chill of alarm that had been there only seconds ago.

From the look on Kayla's pale face, she was

shaken, but aside from that dressing, it looked like she and Sienna were all right. Kayla hadn't seen him yet. Her eyes were fixed on the woman being bundled into the back of the patrol car. Even from here he could see the way shock and strain had drawn Kayla's blanched features into a mask of horror and disbelief. She grew visibly paler at the vitriol being flung at her by the woman as one of the officers closed the back door of the cruiser and the vehicle pulled away. A paramedic moved inside the ambulance, blocking Van's view. As much as it frustrated him, he reminded himself it was okay for now. Kayla was getting the care she needed. The baby was fine. There was nothing else he could do right now but wait.

After another ten minutes he saw Kayla being helped down to the street. He resisted the urge to rush forward. A female officer led Kayla and Sienna back across the street and into the building. He followed them up the stairs.

The front door to what had to be Kayla's apartment was wide open. He stepped through the threshold, his gaze instantly assessing the chaos inside—the overturned side tables, the broken lamp, the cupboard doors hanging open—their shelves denuded of whatever had been inside.

"Sir, this is a crime scene. Please go back downstairs," the officer instructed when she caught sight of him.

"I'm a friend of Ms. Porter's," he repeated, then forced himself to say his next words. "And the father of the baby."

"Is that right, Kayla? Do you want him here?"

Kayla came through a doorway and closed it quietly behind her. The second her eyes lit on him, she seemed to jolt in surprise. Shock, rapidly followed by something else—guilt, probably, he surmised, since she likely knew good and well why he was here—shot across her face.

"Yes, that's okay," she said. She averted her gaze and studiously avoided looking at him again.

The officer turned to Van. "Fine," she said. "You can come in."

He gave the woman a curt nod and moved farther inside, picking his way through the debris to where Kayla stood near an overturned sofa. Shudders racked her body even though the evening air coming through the broken window was pretty mild for May. She was clearly feeling the effects of whatever had transpired here. Looking around, he knew it couldn't have been pleasant. Van shucked off his suit jacket and placed it over her shoulders. She flinched at his touch as his hands briefly rested on her upper arms, but she didn't refuse the warmth his jacket offered.

He waited patiently while she gave her statement, his hands curled into impotent fists as she described the invasion of her home by a woman she'd once trusted. But his interest sharpened at the officer's next words.

"And you say this is the woman who cleared out your bank account last month?"

"I... I can't talk about this right now," she said, glancing at Van, her voice jittering with nerves.

"Don't let me stop you making a full statement," Van responded smoothly. "Give the officer the information she needs."

At his prompting, Kayla carried on, although he sensed she was choosing her words carefully because of him. But no amount of care could disguise the facts, and by the end of her statement he was boiling under the surface. Not only had she brought some homeless person into her apartment, she'd left Sienna with her on a regular basis. Was she completely out of her mind? Van swallowed back the fierce wave of frustration that clogged his throat. He'd just have to bide his time until they were alone so he could have this out with Kayla.

He didn't have to wait much longer before the officer was leaving, with an admonition to Kayla to get her locks changed in the morning.

"I'll take care of it tonight," Van said firmly. "Thank you, officer."

The woman looked from him to Kayla and back again. Then, with a slight nod, she closed the door behind her. Van turned to face Kayla. Silence stretched out between them like a palpable being. He couldn't hold back a moment longer.

"What the hell were you thinking?"

"Tonight? How to stay alive, mostly."

Her attitude did nothing to assuage the burning anger that smoldered deep inside him.

"Nice try, Kayla. You know that's not what I'm talking about. You owe me an explanation and I'm not leaving until I get it."

Three

Kayla righted an armchair and sank into it. She was shattered. If having Zoe return to her apartment, tripping out on the drugs she'd spent all of Kayla's hard-earned savings on, hadn't been enough, now she had to deal with Van, as well?

She swallowed against the sudden dryness in her throat and looked at him. While she might not have been able to see the fury that emanated off him in waves, she could certainly feel it.

"Can't this wait until tomorrow? As you can see, I have a lot on my plate right now."

Her head ached where one of Zoe's missiles had caught her on the forehead and Kayla gingerly touched the dressing the paramedic had put over the cut and closed her eyes. She sensed rather than saw Van move to her side.

"Are you okay? Do you need further medical attention?"

She let her hand drop into her lap and opened her eyes again. "No, I'm okay. It was a glancing blow. Nothing major. I'm just really tired right now. I'm not up for a big argument." She dredged up the last of her courage and fired her next words straight at him. "Perhaps you could call and make an appointment."

He looked startled for a second and then reluctantly amused. But frustration and fury soon took over again. "You're not getting rid of me that easily. You know exactly why I'm here. You owe me answers and I'm not leaving until I get them."

"They'll have to wait until I can get this all sorted out," she said with a weary wave of her hand at the mess that was once her sitting room and kitchen.

"Fine. We do that, then we talk."

"Van, no. It's late, I'm tired and I just want to go to bed."

"Without changing the lock? With that hole in your sliding door?"

She just shook her head, unable to find words. Tonight had been terrifying. When Zoe had shown up, letting herself in with her old key and demanding more money from Kayla, she'd thought she could talk the other woman down. How wrong had she been? Zoe went crazy and grabbed Sienna from her crib, making wild threats. Kayla didn't stop to think. Maternal instinct simply took over and she launched herself at Zoe. Both of them fell onto the bed and she tussled with her, determined to free her little girl from the madwoman's clutches. It was the last thing Zoe had anticipated and Kayla quickly wrested her baby free. After putting Sienna back in her crib, Kayla shoved Zoe out of the bedroom and barricaded them both inside. Sienna screamed her lungs out through the whole ordeal.

Zoe went completely over the edge at that stage and all Kayla could do was listen helplessly while the other woman destroyed the rest of the apartment. She couldn't even call the police, because her phone was in the living room. Thankfully, several of her neighbors had heard the commotion.

Another shudder racked her body. It had been only two days since the implantation procedure. She wasn't supposed to undertake any strenuous activity and things had gotten pretty strenuous when she and Zoe had struggled together—not to mention the strain of dragging her grandmother's old wooden dresser across the door to stop Zoe from breaking her way back into the bedroom. Already she could feel aches and pains in every part of her body. She wrapped her arms across her stomach, holding herself tight. She couldn't lose the babies, not now.

"Kayla?"

Van said her name impatiently, forcing her to drag her thoughts together.

"I'm insured. I'll call someone after I get a hold of the building manager to report the damage," she said weakly.

"And how long do you think it'll take before they can get contractors here? Leave it to me."

Without waiting for her response, Van pulled up a number on his cell phone and started talking. She dropped her head against the back of the chair and closed her eyes again, opening them only when he finished his call.

"A team will be here in about thirty minutes."

He could do that? Just how much pull did he have these days? She didn't want to think about the answer to that question. Van gave her a look, as if he could see exactly what she was thinking.

"You look awful," he said. "Can I get you anything?"

"Sure, a million dollars would be nice, since you're asking," she answered flippantly, then cringed, realizing that probably wasn't going to help her cause.

She hastened to head him off before he verbalized some cutting comeback. "I'm sorry. It's just the shock talking. Maybe..." She turned toward the kitchen, staring at the empty cupboards, some doors hanging drunkenly on their hinges. "I'd have said a cup of tea would be good about now, but she's trashed the kitchen, hasn't she?"

"Leave it to me," Van said again, righting Sienna's high chair on his way through the mess. He picked up her battered electric kettle and held it aloft. "We have progress," he said, then proceeded to rinse it out before refilling it and plugging it back in to heat. While he waited, he started to put things back in the cupboards—what hadn't been smashed to pieces, at least.

"You don't have to do that," she protested.

"You said you'll talk when this is all cleaned up. I'm cleaning up."

The not-so-subtle reminder that he still expected to talk with her tonight did not go unnoticed. While Kayla sipped her tea, Van continued to work through the kitchen, setting it to rights as much as he could. Broken crockery went in a cardboard box. Undamaged food was stacked in the small pantry. Steadily, he restored order. By the time his crew arrived, he was almost done with the kitchen.

Kayla was surprised at the men who came through her front door. One had a prosthetic leg, another severe burn scars down one side of his face and neck, along with several missing fingers. After greeting Van with a camaraderie that obviously went back years, they got to work fast—replacing the shattered pane in her sliding door and putting in new locks. While they worked, Van made and received several calls. Kayla could do nothing but watch and tell them where she wanted the remaining unbroken pieces of furniture set. She thought they were finally all done, but when she saw them begin to install a wireless security system, she started to protest.

"Van, what's that? I don't need some fancy security system and I certainly can't afford it, either."

"Humor me," he said darkly. "Security is my business, and, correct me if I'm wrong, it is my daughter in that bedroom, and those are my children you're carrying, aren't they?"

If she was still carrying them. "Y-yes," she man-

aged to say on the swell of emotion that threatened
to overwhelm her.

It was the first time she'd heard him actually acknowledge the babies as his. The intimation that he'd
take care of them, all of them, was loud and clear. Relief seeped through her whole body. He was going to
help her. Hadn't he just said as much?

It was after midnight when his team finished. Van
saw them to the door and locked it behind them. Double locked and chained, Kayla noted. She fought back
a yawn as Van walked back toward her, pocketing one
set of keys and handing the other set to her.

"You're keeping a set?" she asked, a little confused.

"Let's call it protecting my investment," he said
cryptically.

"Investment?"

"Since you seem to be incapable of looking after
yourself responsibly, obviously it's up to me to do so."

The warm buzz of hope that had filled her only a
short while ago faded fast.

"What exactly do you mean by that?"

"It's too late for me to do anything about the embryo transfer. As much as I vehemently disagree with
what you did, I can't undo it. But I can make sure that
my children are brought up safe."

"That's what I want, too," Kayla agreed.

"Really? And yet you were the one who brought a
stranger in off the street to live with you and Sienna.
A woman whose background you hadn't investigated,

someone with no references. Honestly, Kayla—a drug addict? That's your idea of safe?"

"She wasn't on drugs when I invited her to stay here. And she showed me her qualifications. She is a trained child-care worker and she loved Sienna."

No matter how much she remonstrated, Kayla knew in her heart that Van was right. She trusted people too easily and look where that had left her. Broke and broken.

"Did you know she was suspended from her last place of employment because she failed a drug test—not once but twice?"

Kayla felt sick to her stomach, and not just because she was pregnant. "No, I didn't know that."

"Obviously." Van pushed his fingers through his hair, messing it into a wild tousle that only made him look even more lethal, more attractive, than ever. "I want custody of the children."

"Shared custody, of course. I think it's important that the children get to know their father."

Van cast her a look, his green eyes as deep and unfathomable as a forest lake. "No, Kayla, you misunderstand me. Not shared custody, full custody. It starts with Sienna and will continue with the new babies when they're born."

That sick feeling inside her surged. "You can't mean that. You can't take her away from the only parent she's ever known. It would be cruel. Besides, she's mine. No judge will award you full custody. You signed away your rights already."

"No judge? Really? And when shown your unstable background, your bad choices and your dead-beat friends, do you really think a judge isn't going to look more favorably upon me? Let's see, shall we?" He began to enumerate a few of the escapades she'd gotten caught up in as a teenager, some of which had involved the police.

"Look, everyone makes mistakes when they're young and foolish. Half the population of this country wouldn't have children if what you did as a kid was the only measure of how appropriate a parent you'd be."

"And now, Kayla? You're what, a masseuse?"

He said the word as if she was no more than a street-corner prostitute.

"I'm a fully trained massage therapist. There is a difference, you know. I'm respected and I'm good at my job."

"A job that takes you away from Sienna, right? A job that makes you leave her in the care of someone phenomenally unfit. And tell me, Kayla, does this job of yours pay so well that you can afford to stop work and care for three children under the age of two? Or were you planning to go to the local homeless shelter and find more day-care options there?"

"I'll manage—with your help, of course."

"With my help," he repeated grimly. "You're a piece of work, you know that? How much money do you have left in the bank?"

"That's none of your business."

She'd saved a few hundred dollars since Zoe had cleaned her out. Not much, but it was a start.

"I'm guessing that even if you're saving, it's no-where near enough for you to even make the rent here when you have to stop working after the babies are born, is it?"

"I'll manage. I always have before and I will again. I'll sell Sienna's jewelry if I have to."

Kayla lifted a hand to finger the gold chain at her throat. Van's eyes tracked the movement and she felt the burn of his gaze as if it was a physical touch searing her skin.

"And you think that'll help? And what about when that's all gone—have you thought about that? Be honest with yourself, Kayla. No court is going to declare you a fit parent—especially not in comparison to me. I'm a decorated veteran, a stable and successful businessman, I'm engaged to be married and I have a debt-free home."

He was engaged?

For some reason that one piece of information sent a wave of desolation through her—as though she'd lost something very important without even realizing it. It was stupid, she told herself. It wasn't as if she and Van had ever been close growing up, and that one-night stand the evening after Sienna's funeral had been more of a release of mutual grief than attraction. But even so, she still couldn't look at Van without remembering that night with him. That night she'd wondered if—no, hoped, she finally admitted to herself—they could move forward from that point and discover whether they could have more together.

But he'd run away, hadn't he? Just like he'd done

when he'd turned eighteen and joined the army. Just like he'd done when Sienna's diagnosis had come through and he'd transferred to Special Forces. It seemed that when the chips were down, Van Murphy couldn't be relied upon. So how good a father would he be?

She stood up and squared her shoulders, ignoring the dull throb emanating from her forehead, and looked him in the eye.

"You might think that all it takes is money to be a parent, Van Murphy, but prepare yourself for a monumental fight. A man like you could never be a decent father and my children—yes, *mine*—deserve better than a man who cuts and runs whenever the going gets tough. They deserve love and I'm betting that's something you're never going to be capable of giving to anyone."

Van listened to her words, felt each one like a hot round of lead attempting to pierce the shield he'd wrapped around his emotions a long time ago. She was probably right. The children certainly did deserve more love and affection than he knew how to offer, but the alternative was emphatically not her lackadaisical approach to life, either.

He forced himself to smile. "You haven't changed a bit, have you, Kayla? Still the dreamer, still thinking everything will all work out in the end if you just *believe* in it enough. But life, real life, is not like that."

"Isn't it? Tell me, then, the men you had working for you here tonight. You served with them?"

Where the hell was she going with this? He crossed his arms and nodded.

"And when they came home, they were broken, weren't they. Physically and probably mentally, too."

He grimaced. Those had been bad days.

"And you gave them something, didn't you? You gave them a purpose, gave them back their pride. Because you believed in them, you made them see that they still had skills and worth and something to offer. And they're happy now, aren't they? So don't tell me that things don't work out in the end."

He didn't like the way she made him feel or the way she made him think. He turned and went to the door.

"Yes, that's right, Van. You run away, and you keep on running!" she said forcefully at his retreating back.

From the bedroom, he heard Sienna's cry. "My daughter needs you," he said coldly. "Best you attend to her."

"Yes, that's right. I'm what's best for her and don't you forget it."

He wasn't likely to forget the fierce look on Kayla's pale face, nor the impassioned glare in her eyes. Her expression haunted him as he pounded down the stairs and along the sidewalk toward his car. She was right about his running, he thought as he drove back to the city. But what she didn't understand was that running meant survival. It meant staying safe both physically and emotionally. And if that was what he had to do, then that was what would happen.

He glanced at the time on the dashboard display.

Almost 1:00 a.m. It wouldn't be worth the hour-and-a-half drive south to head to his home. Even if he filed a night flight and took the chopper, he'd no sooner be asleep before he'd need to be up and flying back to San Francisco. He might as well stay in his apartment.

After putting his car in the parking garage in the basement of the building, he took his private elevator up to the apartment. The moment the doors swished open, a tingle of awareness warned him that he wasn't alone.

A single light shone in the sitting room, bathing the woman who curled up in a corner of his sofa in a golden glow. Dani. He wondered how long she'd been waiting here. She must have sensed his arrival because she stretched like a cat and opened her eyes.

"Everything okay?" she asked, getting gracefully to her feet and walking toward him. "I called Imelda to see if you'd gone back to the house tonight but she said you weren't home, so I assumed you'd show up here eventually. Are you happy to see me?"

She lifted her face to his and kissed him. He met her kiss perfunctorily.

"I wasn't expecting you," he said.

She frowned, her mouth a moue of disappointment at his lukewarm reception. "I know, but we're here now, right? We can still make the most of what's left of the night."

Dani lifted her left hand and tucked her hair behind one ear. The movement caused her diamond to flash, reminding him of the decision he'd reached in the car on the way over here. She started to smile invitingly, but when she realized he still wasn't responding in kind, her expression grew serious.

"What is it, Donovan? Is everything okay?"

He sighed. No, everything most certainly was not.

"We need to talk," he said.

"That doesn't sound promising. Can it wait? Maybe things will look better in the morning and…" she arched one brow and gave him a look full of sensual promise "…perhaps I can distract you in the meantime."

Any other day, any other week, he'd have taken her up on the offer. Not after tonight, though, and not after the decision he'd made.

"I'm sorry, Dani—" he started.

"It's her, isn't it?"

"What?"

"The woman with the baby last month. Is it yours?"

Van wiped his face with one hand. This was going to be harder than he thought.

Dani continued. "Of course it is. She's a beautiful child and looks a lot like you. But it doesn't have to be a problem. Everyone can be bought for the right price, Van. Even past lovers. Pay her mother to leave you alone. If you take care of that little problem, we can carry on as we'd always intended."

"It's not as simple as that," Van said.

He explained, in the barest terms possible, about his arrangement with Sienna and about Kayla's decision to have her sister's children—*his* children.

"I don't see the issue. There's no need for you to be

involved in their lives. She came to you for money—
give it to her. Make the problem go away, Donovan."

There was a steely tone to her voice that showed a
side of her he'd always known lingered beneath her
smooth surface. Dani Matthews did not like to be
thwarted. Normally, neither did he. But something
had changed in the course of tonight. Instincts he
hadn't known he possessed had pushed up through
his barriers. Protective instincts, fatherly instincts.

His mother and father had abandoned him in the
pursuit of their next alcoholic buzz. His adoptive
parents had been of the "spare the rod and spoil the
child" variety, never showing love, never admitting
pride in any of his achievements and never, ever, giving encouragement. He wouldn't be like any of them.
He had a chance to make things right for his children.
To give them the stability and the opportunities his
upbringing had never given him.

"No," he said firmly. "I'm sorry, Dani, but our engagement is off. I'm going to be a father."

Four

Kayla lay on the bed staring hard at the screen, willing the sonographer to find that second heartbeat.

"Please," she implored. "Look again."

"Kayla, one out of two is still a good thing. A lot of women don't even progress this far," the woman said encouragingly.

Even though she knew the odds, Kayla couldn't help but feel a sense of devastation that one of her babies hadn't made it.

"You're right, of course," she made herself say in response. "I'm very lucky."

And she kept telling herself that all the way back to work, but the instant she walked into the rooms she shared in a holistic wellness clinic, she felt her hard-fought-for composure begin to crumble. Susan, her boss and fellow therapist at the clinic, took one look at her face and raced forward to envelop Kayla in her arms.

"Oh, hon. Is the news that bad?" she said, sympathetically rubbing Kayla's back.

"I've lost one, Susan. The scan showed only one heartbeat."

"That's still good news, though, isn't it? You have one baby?" Susan loosened her embrace and held Kayla at arm's length. "Look at you. I thought all hope was gone."

Kayla gave her a watery smile. "I'm sorry. I'm just... It's just..."

She couldn't find the words to describe the aching sense of loss—and guilt—that had settled deep inside her. Every time she argued with herself that there was nothing she could have done differently to ensure the success of both the embryos, she was reminded of that night with Zoe. Of how physical it had gotten. Of how all of that was her fault. *She'd* brought Zoe into her home, into her and Sienna's world. *She'd* left her phone on the coffee table, open to her internet banking. *She'd* done nothing about changing her locks after Zoe had left.

No matter which way she looked at it, it was all her fault. She felt like she'd failed—both the lost embryo and her sister. The day had started bad enough when, before she left for the scan this morning, the papers had arrived from Van's lawyers; he was suing for custody of Sienna. It felt like an assault on her right to be Sienna's mother and the mother of the babies— no, baby, she corrected herself—she carried and she had nothing to fight it with. Tears filled her eyes and began to roll helplessly down her cheeks.

"There, there, hon. Don't take on so. Must be all those hormones heading into overdrive in your body, hmm? Why don't you take the rest of the day off? You only have three bookings. I'll cover for you, okay?"

Kayla reluctantly accepted Susan's offer. She couldn't really afford to take extra time off, not when she was so financially strapped, but right now the idea of working and investing what was left of her energy into other people was just too much for her. Sienna was in day care until five o'clock, so she decided to let her stay there and headed to her apartment. She hadn't been sleeping all that well. Maybe she could just take a nap and be in a better headspace to figure out her next move.

She'd been dozing on her sofa for a couple of hours when she heard a knock at the door. Still fuzzy, she got to her feet and rubbed her face, surprised to find her fingers came away wet. She'd been crying even in her sleep. The reality of it all hit her again. There was another knock at the door.

"Kayla? I know you're in there."

Van. Of course it had to be him. The man had the worst timing in the world. She dragged herself to the door.

"I'm not really up for visitors right now. Can you come another time?" she said at the solid block of wood with its shiny new locks.

"This isn't a social call. Open up."

"Look, if you're wondering if your papers got here today, they did. Okay? You can go now."

"I'm here because I'm worried about you," he interrupted. "Now open the door."

Kayla's shoulders drooped as emotion swelled through her again. He was worried about her? Worried about his progeny, more like. She had no doubt that she was nothing but a peripheral thought to him. She slipped the chain off, twisted the two locks open and swung the door wide.

"Come in," she said listlessly.

She hadn't been kidding when she said she wasn't up to visitors, but most especially, she wasn't up to him. She turned her back on him to head back to the couch, but not before she caught a whiff of his cologne. Funny how it didn't make her stomach twist and revolt like so many other scents already did. The fragrance summed him up perfectly with its masculine woody blend and sharper citrus top note, and it reminded her anew of the difference between this man and the boy she'd known growing up—not to mention the man she'd sought oblivion with after Sienna's funeral.

Van came in, locked the door behind him and came to stand by the sofa, where she'd reassumed her position lying down under a soft blanket. His eyes raked her, almost as if he was trying to see inside her.

"I went to see you at work," he started.

Kayla felt her spirits dip even lower. Susan was a lovely woman but confidentiality was a foreign concept to her. She'd have told Van everything. His next words confirmed it.

"Your boss told me one of the embryos didn't take." He paused a moment, took in a deep breath. "Will you be all right? Is there anything I can do?"

"No, there's nothing anyone can do. It happens. I was half expecting it but I still… I still hoped, you know?"

Van moved around the room. Kayla surreptitiously watched him from her supine position on the sofa. He carried himself straight and tall, using every inch of his six-foot-two frame to fill the space he occupied. And all around him, like some cape imbued with superpowers, he wore an air of suppressed energy. As if he was coiled, ready to strike at a moment's notice. As if nothing and no one would ambush or surprise him. He'd always been like that, even as a kid—except, when it was just her and Sienna, he'd sometimes let his guard down. She guessed it was only natural that the army had enhanced this hyperawareness in him. But he wasn't in a war zone now—unless you counted the legal attack he'd launched on her this morning.

The reminder made her swing her legs to the floor and sit up straight.

"What do you want, Van? To see I'm okay? You've seen me. You can leave now."

"Tell me about the scan," he demanded, settling into the chair opposite and leaning toward her, his elbows resting on the tops of his thighs and his hands loosely clasped. "What's it like? What did you see?"

She briefly outlined the procedure and told him about the indistinct image on the screen.

"You really can't see a lot. It's still early days," she finished.

"But the sonographer heard a heartbeat?"

"I did, too."

He leaned back against the chair and thrust his hands through his hair. "Wow."

"Like I said, it's still early days."

Yes, there had been a heartbeat, but that could still change. There was a long time before the fetus would be considered viable. Right now it didn't even look like a baby—the scan had just been a collection of light and dark shapes to her—but the audio had confirmed the baby was there. She needed to hold on to that, take joy in that confirmation. It wasn't like her to be downcast, and she hated it, but she was mourning the missing heartbeat—and with it, mourning her sister all over again.

Van was unaccustomed, these days, at least, to feeling helpless. He was the kind of man who took action. He served, he protected, he saved. That he had virtually no control over any of this situation with Kayla was enough to drive a man to drink—except he didn't drink anymore. Ever. Not since he'd learned the truth about his parents. Actually, no, his decision had come earlier than that. It started in the cold gray dawn after that night with Kayla, after her sister's funeral. A night when they'd had too much to drink and then— He shut down the thought before it could form fully in his mind. No, he did dumb things when he'd been drinking—made dumb choices. No more.

Of course, it looked like the dumbest decision he'd ever made was agreeing to be Sienna's donor. But then, he'd never expected things to turn out like this. Now he had a kid and another on the way.

It was his worst nightmare come true but he had to take control to make sure their childhoods wouldn't be the disaster zone his had been. They needed a strong role model, someone who could guide them into being good human beings who made the right choices in life. He had to be that person no matter how many times he'd told himself he couldn't, or wouldn't, raise kids of his own.

He had an ethical obligation to see that his children had the best of everything—morally and materially. That meant being the best damn father he could be. His kids would have a solid, safe, reliable upbringing. And no matter what impractical ideas Kayla had about parenting, he'd made himself a promise—he'd be the one making the hard decisions in their lives. He'd be the one keeping them safe, now and in the future. If that meant making sure their birth mother was cared for 24/7 until the new baby was born, then that was what he'd do.

Kayla needed his help right now, and she was going to get it—even though he knew she'd fight him on this. But what she probably hadn't counted on was that in the last several years he'd become quite used to succeeding—in everything. He wasn't about to stop now and he wasn't above using some heavy emotional leverage to achieve his objective, either.

He picked his next words very carefully. "You know, you don't need to make things so hard on yourself."

She made a noise that fell somewhere between a snort and a laugh. "Really? That's rather ironic, when you're the one making things hard on me."

Kayla leaned forward and gave the legal envelope sitting in front of her on the coffee table a dismissive shove toward him with her fingertips. He ignored it and the quick surge of frustration that threatened to cloud his thinking.

"I mean, you don't need to do this all on your own," he rephrased.

"Oh, you think I should just give in to your demands? Hand Sienna over to you without another thought? Forget I carried her in my body, birthed her, nurtured her and raised her on my own these past ten months? Forget that she's my sister's baby and that I promised to raise her?"

Her voice wobbled, betraying her vulnerability. Out of nowhere came the urge to wrap her in his arms, to tell her that everything was going to be okay. It was most inconvenient. He didn't want to feel that way toward her. He didn't want to feel that way toward anybody. He'd drilled that sap out of himself, taught himself not to feel anything more than he wanted to feel when he wanted to feel it. He compartmentalized and planned; he didn't wing it. He made decisions based on analysis and structure, not emotion. He did not offer hugs to tearful females, even if they were carrying his kids.

Again, the unwelcome impulse to comfort her

fought to rise to the surface. Again, he shoved it straight back down. It was time to bring in the big guns—he might not want to feel emotion but he wasn't above manipulating it to get what he wanted.

"Sienna wouldn't have wanted you to do this on your own, Kayla. You know that. You said yourself that she would have wanted me to be a part of this, to help you, to support you."

"To support me, yes. Not to rip everything I hold dear away from me."

Her face grew taut, her throat worked—swallowing almost convulsively—and he saw the stricken echo of sorrow reflect from her blue eyes. He averted his gaze. Damn, he couldn't have felt any worse right now if he'd just kicked a puppy. What was it with these feelings? Was she leaking hormones in the air or something? He had to move, to get out of the line of fire. He shoved up and out of his chair and started to pace, talking all the time—enumerating all the reasons it would be a good idea for her to accept his offer of household help, financial security, comfortable living. You name it, he'd provide it. Help to infinity and beyond. After all, hadn't that been her objective all along when she'd come to see him last month? Wasn't he giving her, albeit belatedly, exactly what she'd asked for?

When he finally wound down, her expression was more normal again. Granted, she was still pale and her eyes still red rimmed, but there was a light of battle in them again. A light that reminded him of old Kayla. The one who got a harebrained idea in that head of hers and went off, damning the consequences without a second thought—just like she had with this pregnancy.

"So you're saying I should give up the lease on this apartment, give up a job I love, move south to your no doubt obscenely luxurious home on the hills outside Monterey, hand over Sienna to some faceless nanny and spend my time growing your next child like some uninvolved incubator until it's born, whereupon you plan to take it and my daughter and show me the door? I don't think so."

He knew it wouldn't be easy. "Look, sure, when you present it like that, it doesn't sound appealing, I agree. But ask yourself this—what's your other option? How are you going to cope, pregnant and working without any help? Your friend Susan, she told me how sick you were with Sienna. What did she call it? Hyper-something-or-other."

"Hyperemesis gravidarum," Kayla supplied.

"Yeah, that. What if you get that again?"

"I'd already started by now with Sienna. Maybe I won't get sick this time. Maybe everything will go textbook perfect."

She was grasping at straws. "My research shows that if you've had it before, you have an 86 percent chance of developing it again in a subsequent pregnancy."

"Your research." She shook her head and huffed that snort-laugh again. "You did what? Googled it?" She gave him a slow clap. "Well done, Van. Well done."

He felt hot color rise in his cheeks. "Even if it only lasts through your first trimester, how do you expect to work during that? And Sienna, let's not forget her needs—not to mention bodily functions. Can you really see yourself coping with all that on your own?"

"Of course I can. I'll do whatever I have to."

"You don't get it, do you? You need help. *My* help."

"On your terms," she said bitterly.

"My kids, my terms."

"You forget—I have custody, legally and figuratively, of your supposed kids."

He bent down and pushed the legal envelope back toward her across the table.

"But for how much longer, Kayla?"

He stared at her, secretly surprised that she was fighting him this hard. She'd never wanted children before. Her life had always been one adventure after another. Backpacking in Kathmandu. Hiking in Papua New Guinea. Digging for opals in Australia. The antithesis of her sister, she'd never wanted to be tied down to anything or anyone. The only permanent tie in her life had been to Sienna—and he knew that was what was driving this stubbornness now. She'd made a promise to her sister. But surely she knew that Sienna would have wanted her children to have a safe and stable home. He could provide that. Kayla couldn't. He doubted she truly wanted to. She'd always been such a free spirit—surely she couldn't have changed that much. He tried another tack.

"Look, it doesn't have to be like this. You don't have to keep fighting me. I'll pay you for the surrogacy—for Sienna and for this child. Then you can go forth and do whatever it is that you do."

"No. *These are my children.* I'm not abandoning them and especially not to you. You've already discarded them once, when you tried to stop me from undergoing the procedure. You're just as likely to forsake them again when the going gets rough or when you start to feel too much. It's what you always do."

Her words hurt, but he pushed back the pain like he always did. "Things have changed. *I've* changed."

"And what about your fiancée? Does she welcome this opportunity to have a ready-made family? One where she doesn't have to be involved in any of the messy stuff like nausea, stretch marks or giving birth?"

"Dani and I are no longer engaged," he said bluntly.

Dani had fought hard that night to change his mind about their engagement but he'd been adamant. They continued to work together because neither of them were about to let a broken engagement get in the way of a perfectly good business merger, but he knew she thought he was crazy to want to take on his children.

"Why?" Kayla demanded. "Did she want too much from you, Van? Make you feel too much, perhaps?"

"We had our reasons," he answered. There was no way he was going into the details with Kayla.

"And I have mine now," she was quick to retort.

"So, we're at an impasse."

She crossed her arms and looked up at him. "We certainly are."

Van shoved his hand through his hair again and took a couple of steps away before wheeling around.

"We both know I'll win custody. What if I'm prepared to discuss some kind of visitation after the children are born?"

"Visitation?" She gave him a scornful look. "Please don't insult me like that. You know that's not enough. These are *my* children—in every way."

"In every way except biologically."

Their eyes locked in a silent duel, but he was a master at this and he'd stared down far more determined enemies before today. She was the first to look away.

"Okay, fine," she said bitterly. "I'll consider your offer."

"Seriously consider it?" he pressed.

"I said I would, didn't I?"

He studied her face, checked her hands to make sure she hadn't crossed her fingers, as she used to when she was a kid. She appeared to be telling the truth. He'd have to take it.

"I'll be back at the end of the week for your answer."

His words caused a fissure in her carefully composed facade.

"The end of the week? But that's only a couple of days!" she objected.

"It's all I'm prepared to concede. If I don't have your answer by then, I'll be instructing my lawyers to fast-track my petition for custody of Sienna."

He stalked to the door.

"You can't do that to me. It's not right," she protested.

"I can't? Just watch me."

Five

Kayla went about her treatment room, making sure everything was ready for her next appointment. She was exhausted, the tiredness of early pregnancy and caring for Sienna taking a toll she hadn't expected, and the severe nausea she'd experienced with Sienna's pregnancy had asserted itself over the weekend with a vengeance.

But she'd work things out. She just had to. One of her girlfriends had flippantly suggested crowdfunding to help her get through this—even if it was only to raise the funds to fight Van through family court. She had to admit, the idea had briefly held appeal, but wouldn't that just be grasping at straws? And how would it look to a judge? She had no doubt that

Van would use such a thing as yet another example of why she wasn't a fit parent.

She put her hands at the base of her spine and leaned backward, stretching out her lower back before straightening her shoulders and heading to Reception to welcome her next client. She heard voices as she approached—a male murmur followed by an almost flirtatious giggle from Susan. Then the male voice again, this time sounding so familiar that a ripple of nausea lurched from the pit of her stomach, making her falter in her tracks.

She rested a hand on her diaphragm and swallowed, closing her eyes just a moment. Opening them again, she reoriented herself. No, she couldn't possibly have just heard Van's voice. Not here. The clinic was primarily frequented by convalescent patients needing massage therapy, and Van was most definitely not convalescent. Kayla drew in a steadying breath and completed the short distance down the corridor.

"Ah, here she is," Susan said brightly as Kayla entered the reception area.

Van gave Kayla an assessing look. "Here she is indeed," he said in a voice that told her he was here for answers.

She swallowed again, but it did nothing to ease the unsettled feeling that racked her. His deadline had come and gone, and to avoid speaking to him, she'd studiously ignored her phone and had gone so far as to go and visit with a friend up the coast over the weekend just in case he came to her apartment.

She might have known he'd track her down at work when he didn't get the answer he sought.

"Mr. Murphy," she said, acknowledging his presence with a short nod. "Can I help you?"

"I hope so. I have this pain in my neck." He made no attempt to gesture to any strained muscles, just keeping his eyes trained on her like a rifle scope and leaving her in no doubt as to what the source of his apparent pain was.

"We specialize in convalescent therapy here. I can't help you."

Kayla heard Susan's sharply indrawn breath. She'd never been rude to a client before.

"Mr. Murphy, please excuse us a moment," Susan said smoothly.

She cast Van a smile and took Kayla by the arm into a small side office.

"What are you doing?" she demanded. "I know you've told me about your problems with him but if the man wants his neck massaged, then you massage his neck."

"That's not what he's here for," Kayla protested.

"This is your place of work," Susan reminded her emphatically. "Not your personal battlefield. Now, I suggest you take him through to your treatment room and get to work."

Without waiting for her response, Susan left the office and returned to Reception.

"Thanks for your support," Kayla muttered under her breath before following her. She forced herself to smile at Van. "Please, come with me."

He smiled back at her, satisfied that he'd won this round. In her room, she directed him to remove his tie and shirt and to lie facedown on the table. Once he was in position, she moved to the head of the bed and, with oil-slicked hands, began to stroke the muscles of his shoulders and neck. She tried to ignore how his body felt beneath her palms and any thoughts of the last time she'd touched his bare skin.

He was still strong but perhaps not as heavily muscled as he'd been back then, before he'd mustered out of the army. But stroking his skin now brought back memories she'd rather forget. Memories of how well they'd fit together, of the pleasure they'd wrought from one another's bodies. Of the glimmer of hope that maybe things had changed between them, that they could forge a new relationship together—one as adults who could be good for one another instead of the children and teenagers who'd so often butted heads. But then she reminded herself of the devastation she'd felt when she'd realized, come morning, that he'd gone without another word.

She applied more pressure—working her fingertips into the stiffness of his shoulders. Working out some of the frustration and helplessness she felt from right now as well as from back then. He needed it, anyway—while the appointment might have been a ruse to force her to talk to him, the knots in his muscles were crying out for attention.

Under normal circumstances she would have spent more time warming up the muscles of her clients, who were generally weaker and older. But Van got no such consideration. For this moment, she could kid herself she had the upper hand on this man. She hated being manipulated, and he knew it.

"Could you enjoy this a little less," he grunted from the table.

"You came here for a therapeutic massage, didn't you?" she reminded him, putting extra pressure on a particularly hard knot of muscle. "You carry a lot of tension here. You should try relaxing a bit more."

"I'll relax when you give me your answer. Why have you been avoiding me?"

She started to speak, to lie and say she needed more time, but she knew that would be a waste of breath. He'd made it clear when they'd last seen each other that she had only a couple of days to make up her mind, and while she hadn't wanted to admit it at the time, she had already made her decision before he even pulled away from the curb outside her apartment. She just didn't like that she'd had to make it, or that it favored him. The crowdfunding idea had been fun to bat around with her friend but she'd known all along that it wouldn't work. Without her savings she had only one option left.

"Kayla?" he prompted.

"Sienna and I went away for the weekend. It was a preexisting arrangement."

"I see. So rather than tell me that, you thought you'd just make me wait? Make me wonder if you'd skipped town altogether? You realize that avoiding me like that would have endangered your case, don't you? Sienna is the subject of a custody dispute. A good lawyer could make a case that what you'd done could be construed as abduction." He paused before adding, "I have very good lawyers."

Kayla stiffened, ready to argue—but decided against rising to the bait. It would just be a delaying tactic. She couldn't push back this conversation any longer.

"I'm sorry," she said, shifting and focusing her attention on a different section of his back. He groaned as she found another knot and began to work it out. "But if it's any consolation, I have reached a decision."

She felt him stiffen beneath her hands, probably undoing all her hard work.

"And?" he asked.

"I have a few conditions."

"Of course you do." The sarcasm of his words hung in the air. "Come on, then. Spit them out."

"I will consider a fifty-fifty shared custody agreement. In return, you will cover all my pre- and postnatal costs of a medical and personal nature."

"Personal?"

She bit back a smile. She'd been scrimping and saving every penny for the last five years so that she could support the children she planned to have. If Van was willing to throw all that money at lawyers to drag her through family court, he shouldn't mind using some of his seemingly endless funds to let her pamper herself a bit for a change. It wasn't a deal breaker, of course, but it would be a nice benefit to repay her for being cooperative. "Well, I'll need a new wardrobe, for a start."

"Why do I feel like you're not taking this seriously?" he muttered.

"Oh, I'm definitely serious."

Van slowly counted to ten and forced himself to relax, not an easy thing to do when she seemed hellbent on extracting as much discomfort from his muscles as she possibly could. Hell, and people regularly paid for this? But, he reminded himself, he was a step closer to getting exactly what he wanted. He needed to go softly.

"Anything else?" he asked, forcing his voice to remain civil.

"When you present my mandates to me in an acceptable document, I'll think about doing what you want."

"And you'll agree to give up work and move into my house?"

He could feel her tiring already. This work was intensely physical. Even he could see that she wouldn't be able to sustain the energy she needed to do this for long into her pregnancy.

"I'll need to work out notice, but, yes, if that's what it takes."

She was beaten and she knew it. He wanted to punch the air and shout "Hooah!" but he knew when to take his victories like a man.

"I'll see to the paperwork. Do you have a doctor already? Your records will need to be transferred to someone closer to home."

"I'll give you the information you need before you go today."

She leaned into the strokes she worked along his back now, putting her entire body weight into the massage. Now that she wasn't intent on punishing him, it felt great—a little too great. He reasserted control over his body, forcing every part of him to relax, to stop fighting her mentally and physically. He had what he wanted. Her motions grew lighter, gentler, and then, after the merest pressure at the base of his spine, she wiped his back with a warmed towel and then he heard her step away from the table.

"That's it—you're done. You can get up when you're ready."

He heard the clink of a glass and the sound of running water as he rolled over and got up. She handed him the water.

"Here—you'll need to drink. The last thing you need is a toxic headache."

He accepted the glass, noting that now that the massage was over, she assiduously avoided touching him. She turned and he watched as she consulted her phone and then transferred a name and details onto a piece of paper.

"There, my obstetrician's details."

He glanced at the small sheet before pocketing it. "When will you move in?"

"You haven't presented me with the agreement yet."

"Still hedging, Kayla?"

She sighed. "I guess. I don't like giving up my independence, and aside from that, I'm not convinced this is going to be the best thing for any of us."

How could it not be? "You say you have to work out notice here. What's that—a month? Two weeks?"

"A month," she confirmed. "And I need to give my landlord a month's notice, too."

"I'll see to it that the agreement is delivered to you tomorrow morning. You'll be here?"

She nodded. "I have a full day, so, yes, I'll be here."

He studied her a moment. In every line of her body, she looked defeated.

"It's not a prison sentence, Kayla. You won't regret this."

She returned his gaze just as steadily. "I already do but I don't really have a choice, do I?"

He could lie to her, but he wouldn't. "No, you don't."

"You know the way out," she said, turning her back to him.

He waited a few more seconds, feeling somehow at a disadvantage. He should have been filled with a sense of victory. He had exactly what he'd asked for, albeit with an amendment regarding custody. And that wasn't really so much of a hurdle—sooner or later Kayla was bound to show her true, irresponsible colors. When that happened, it would be easy enough for him to press for full custody. If her wanderlust kicked in again, she might even give it up without a fight. This was all working out perfectly.

So why did he feel like he'd lost something even bigger?

Six

It shouldn't have been this easy to just pack up one life and move to another, Kayla thought as her car rounded a curve in the road. Still, she'd spent most of her life reinventing herself and moving on to new pastures, hadn't she? She had to look at this as simply another adventure. As she pulled up outside the address, she turned back to check on Sienna, who'd been awake for most of the journey from their apartment to this aerie overlooking the Pacific Ocean.

Kayla wasn't generally impressed by what she'd always deemed excesses of grandeur but this place was really something. Through massive iron gates, she spied the house—a double-storied Mediterranean-inspired mansion. Her heart began to hammer in her chest. Van lived *here*?

The property looked huge—certainly far too big for a man living on his own. Maybe things wouldn't be so bad after all. In a house this size, it would be easy not to have to see him.

The building itself was imposing yet welcoming at the same time. Situated as it was at the top of the hill, it would command an impressive view of the ocean, and even though it looked isolated in its setting, it was still relatively close to both Monterey and Carmel. He had the best of everything, didn't he? And now he had her and Sienna, too.

In front of her, the gates began to open.

"Looks like this is us," Kayla commented, putting her old Toyota into gear and driving through.

She looked back in her rearview mirror and saw the gates slide closed behind them. The sensation of feeling trapped fluttered against the periphery of her mind. *Don't be stupid*, she told herself. *This is the best thing for Sienna and the baby. If it wasn't, you wouldn't be here.* Van had been right about the physical toll her pregnancy would put on her body and her ability to continue working. Once the hyperemesis gravidarum had hit, she'd been unable to handle being around so many different people with all the various scents they carried with them, not to mention the aromatic oils they used in the clinic. Susan had managed to find another therapist to take on her position and had released her from her notice with good wishes for her future. Even though she could have moved to Van's house earlier, she'd stubbornly stayed on at the apartment until the very last day of her lease.

Kayla rolled to a halt near the front entrance. A movement there alerted her to Van's presence. Even from here she could see the concern painted on his face. It struck her that she should probably have let him know that a diaper change for Sienna midjourney had led to a severe bout of nausea for her that had forced her to take a long driving break. It had taken almost an hour before she could keep down a few sips of water and they'd been able to head on their way again. One of the worst things about being this sick through her pregnancy was that she'd had to wean Sienna rather abruptly, too. She barely kept enough fluid down to stop herself from becoming dehydrated, let alone enough to be able to continue to nurse.

Before she could even turn off her ignition, he had her door open.

"Did you have trouble on the way? I tried to call you."

"I'm sorry. I forgot to charge my phone before we left and we had to stop on the way."

She neglected to include her reasons for stopping, not wanting Van to lord her frailty over her again. Although he was unaware of just how sick she'd been, he'd still been reluctant to let her drive herself, but she'd been adamant, holding on to every last second of independence—and it hadn't been fun at all. She felt his gaze rake over her, sensed he wasn't happy.

He cleared his throat and offered her his hand. "It isn't important now. You're here and that's what matters."

There was a possessive note in his voice that made

her give him a second glance. The lines of worry had already begun to fade from Van's face as he helped her from the car. He was dressed more casually than she was used to seeing him and for a moment she was reminded of the old Van. But the old Van didn't exist anymore, she told herself as she moved to the rear passenger door to release Sienna from her car seat. And this version, in a pair of well-washed jeans that were faded in all the right places and a T-shirt that fit his muscled shoulders just a little too snugly, was an unknown quantity. One that was equally as unsettling as he was infuriating.

Van gently elbowed her aside. "Here, let me do that."

"It's okay. She's just woken and she's not used to you yet. She might cry."

"She'll have to get used to me sooner or later," he said, pulling open the door on Sienna's side and reaching in to unsnap the child restraints.

Kayla stood back, the impact of his words sinking in. She'd been so focused on finishing up at work and packing and sorting her things for going into storage that she hadn't looked past moving day. This was to be her new reality—their new home, together—at least until the new baby was weaned. The somber finality of the thought brought back that trapped feeling she'd experienced just a few minutes ago. She pressed one hand to her lower belly and drew in a deep breath.

In the process of lifting a surprisingly amenable Sienna from her car seat, Van turned his head to look at Kayla. His brows drew into a frown.

"Are you okay? You're a bit pale."

"Always telling me how great I look, Van," she said with an attempt to lighten his intensity. "I'm just tired, that's all."

"You should have let me drive you, like I offered. Or at least allowed me to provide you with a driver."

"Self-sufficient to the core, that's me," she emphasized and gave a reassuring smile to Sienna, who was looking from Van to Kayla and back again. "Besides, I can't really see you driving that," she said, gesturing to her dented but generally reliable car.

"I don't want to see *you* driving that," he commented with a disparaging glance at the car.

The baby looked uncertain about the man holding her, but when Van held her close and smiled at her, she answered with a reciprocal, albeit slightly more gummy, grin. Kayla watched him with interest and saw the exact moment that he became captivated by his daughter. The two locked gazes. Suddenly the expression in Van's green eyes deepened, as if he'd just realized something incredibly important, and his smile took on a tenderness that hadn't been there before. Sienna reached up and patted his cheek, a little chortle of delight escaping as she felt the stubble on his cheeks against her tiny palms.

Instead of feeling relief that at least Sienna wasn't about to throw a screaming fit at being held by a stranger, a curious sense of loss filtered through Kayla. Was this what she'd really been fighting all along? The truth that she would be sharing Sienna's affections with Van? Surely, she wasn't that petty—was she? Maybe she was, she forced herself to admit. Maybe both she and Van needed to make some major adjustments. The idea was a difficult fit and certainly not one she embraced.

Van pressed a kiss to Sienna's head, then looked up. "Come on inside, I'll get Jacob to put your car in the garage later. Just leave the keys in the ignition."

Kayla raised her eyebrows. "You have staff?"

Van cracked a half smile in her direction. "Does that make me a capitalist pig? If so, I'm sorry, but, yes, I have staff. Jacob, who takes care of the cars and the grounds, Imelda, his wife, who looks after the house and meals, and now, Annabelle, who will be helping you with Sienna."

"A nanny?" She couldn't keep the shock and irritation from her voice. "I told you when I signed your agreement, I don't need a nanny."

"*Our* agreement," he corrected. "Just think of her as a precautionary measure."

"Is this another attempt to undermine my position as Sienna's mom? Or are you planning ahead, hoping she'll transfer her affections to another woman so that when I'm forced to share custody with you, she won't miss me so much?"

"Jeez, Kayla, relax. Annabelle is here to help you—to take care of the day-to-day things that will become harder for you as time progresses, especially if you don't start to feel better soon. She comes well recommended and worked for years as a pediatric nurse before becoming a nanny. Whatever your feelings about me, don't judge her until you meet her, okay?"

"I'm ten weeks now. I should start to feel better anytime soon. Besides, I'm responsible for Sienna's care and I don't see why that should change just because I'm pregnant." She sniffed indignantly. "If you want this Annabelle to have a highly paid holiday in your luxury home, go ahead. No skin off my nose. I only hope she doesn't get bored."

Van laughed. Honest-to-goodness laughed from deep in his belly. It made Sienna's eyes open wide, before she too chuckled along with him. Feeling like little more than an outsider with her own dysfunctional little family, Kayla wrapped her arms around herself.

"I don't see what is so funny," she said stiffly.

Van was still smiling when he spoke. "Most women I know with kids would love to have a nanny to help out. Tell me you're not just being possessive about the time Annabelle will be spending with Sienna."

The way he phrased it, it sounded like a foregone conclusion that this Annabelle would be taking over Sienna's care. It also made Kayla sound like a bit of a brat.

"I'm her mother. It's only natural that I would be uncomfortable about yet another *stranger*," she said with a sharp look at Van that hopefully left him in no doubt that she lumped him in that same category, "taking care of my daughter."

"And yet you were happy to leave her with a drug addict in your own home?" Van replied equally piercingly.

"I didn't know—"

"You can rest assured that very thorough checks

were made into Annabelle's suitability as a caregiver for Sienna. Now, if you've quite finished grandstanding over things you can't change, let's go inside."

Van started toward the front door with Sienna in his arms. Torn between stamping her foot in frustration and following him, she chose the latter.

Kayla was so ruffled she almost didn't notice the opulent entrance of Van's home, but a slight wave of dizziness caused her to pause in her steps as she crossed the threshold in Van's wake. She'd heard the phrase *take your breath away* a time or two and had thought it hugely appropriate when faced with the majestic vistas that nature provided during her world travels, but she had to admit that the foyer to Van's house was certainly spectacular. The double front doors opened into a two-storied and spacious tiled entrance. From where she stood, she saw a massive staircase with an ornate balustrade swirling to the upper level, and directly ahead, she spied a formal sitting room with wide floor-to-ceiling windows that opened out onto a terrace on the other side.

She took a few steps forward. Light spilled in through the windows, making everything look fresh and spacious and gilded, while the pale gold tile floor gave it an inviting warmth. To one side she glimpsed a formal dining room, to the other what looked like a wood-paneled library.

"I can't believe you have all this house for just one person. Oh, and staff," she added, the last part heavily weighted with derision.

"It's home," Van answered plainly. "You know

what I came from. I promised myself that when I could, I would have the best of everything. I have it now."

He hadn't said a lot but Kayla felt as though she'd been very firmly put in her place. It made her feel as if her snide remarks had been both nasty and unnecessary. She was so busy focusing on what she perceived to be his materialistic overindulgence she'd forgotten where he'd come from. What he'd endured. His simple summation of this house being home struck her hard. She was about to apologize when Van continued.

"You're probably imagining how many homeless people you could fit in here, right?"

"It crossed my mind," she admitted.

"You don't have to live on the streets to be homeless," Van gestured through to an archway. "Come through here and meet Imelda. She'll give you two something to eat before showing you the house. Don't worry about your things. Jacob will bring them in shortly."

"Van?"

He paused in the archway, father and daughter perfectly framed and driving home to her just how much her life and Sienna's would change from this day forward.

"I'm sorry for being such a bitch."

He shrugged and didn't say anything, but his eyes never left her face. She felt her cheeks heat under his perusal. He and Sienna looked perfect together, both dark haired and green eyed. No one seeing them could doubt their fundamental connection to one another. Again, she felt as though she was the outsider, peripheral to everyone's needs. The sensation lasted until Sienna thrust out her chubby little arms and said, "Mamma!"

It galvanized Kayla into action and she reached for her daughter. *Her* daughter, she reminded herself, no matter the little girl's biological ties to the man holding her. Sienna was the child of Kayla's heart, as was the baby steadily growing inside her. She didn't need a legal agreement to know that. She took Sienna in her arms and felt a sense of rightness, of spiritual balance, ease through her.

Van continued to watch her. "I realize this is upsetting for you, Kayla, but it's for the best. For everyone."

"Sometimes it's just a bit hard to see that," she admitted, nuzzling the top of Sienna's head and immediately regretting it as her nose filled with the scent of the baby's shampoo. She swallowed back the fresh wave of nausea that threatened.

It was ridiculous to suddenly feel bereft when Sienna transferred to Kayla's arms, Van told himself, and yet it gave him some insight as to how she was probably feeling about having someone else step in to be Sienna's parent when she was used to having her daughter to herself.

"Yeah, well, we both have a lot of adjusting to do," he commented.

For him, everything so far had been about the logistics of getting them here. The legal agreement, getting confirmation that Kayla had indeed relinquished the lease on her apartment and given notice at her work. None of those were things he could ultimately control, and despite what he'd said, he found that now that the shock of discovering he was a father had worn away, he had no desire to make Kayla's life truly difficult. He simply had to do what was best for his children.

In the kitchen, he introduced Kayla to Imelda, who cooed over the baby with glee. He could see Kayla begin to relax by increments.

"Isn't she just a love?" Imelda said with a doting smile. "And so like her daddy. Oh, that reminds me. Mr. Murphy, your Little Brother will be here tomorrow morning as arranged. He rang to confirm while you were outside."

"Little brother?" Kayla asked, looking at him in surprise.

"Well, not his real little brother," Imelda continued without missing a beat before Van could reply. "He's involved in the Big Brothers Big Sisters organization as a mentor. Young Alex has no dad and when he started to get into trouble at school, his mom knew he needed a strong male role model to help her guide him. Ben's gone from being a truant to an A-plus student since he's been matched with Mr. Murphy. You should see them together. You'd think they were both twelve year olds when they're in the pool. I swear my Jacob has to top it up every time Alex comes to visit."

"I can imagine," Kayla murmured absently.

"And Alex is just going to adore this young lady, here," Imelda continued, chucking Sienna under her chin.

Van felt his cell phone vibrate in his pocket, reminding him he still had work to attend to.

"Imelda, could you give these two ladies something to eat and then show them their rooms? I need to check in with the office but I'll be down for dinner."

Before he could leave the kitchen, however, Kayla bristled again.

"Rooms? Sienna has always slept in the same room as me. I don't want her to be more unsettled than necessary," Kayla remonstrated.

He sighed. Did everything have to be a battle with her?

"Your rest is vitally important. Annabelle is scheduled to take on night duties as required. Honestly, Kayla, have you seen yourself lately? You look like you could do with a decent night's sleep. How about you see if Sienna will settle in a room of her own first? If it distresses her, we'll move her in with you."

Kayla stared back at him and for a moment he thought she might argue, but then she seemed to weaken, her entire body drooping as if she'd had all the wind taken out of her sails.

"That sounds reasonable," she answered woodenly.

He reached out and put a hand on her shoulder. "Thank you, Kayla. I mean that."

He knew how much it must have cost her to give in to him on any point, especially on something that meant she'd have less time with Sienna. But he was adamant. She really did look worn out and it made him feel guilty, even though he'd checked on her frequently by telephone. He should have been following up with her face-to-face this past month, but due to having to personally oversee a security installation overseas, he hadn't had an opportunity to visit her—and he hadn't made one, either, a little voice reminded him.

So what if he was trying to avoid conflict? She'd insisted everything was going fine, that she was fine, that the baby was fine—it had gotten to the stage where if he heard the word *fine* one more time, he thought he'd tear his hair out. But it was clear everything was not fine. She was pale and thinner than he remembered and exhaustion shadowed her eyes. If he'd had any qualms about coercing her into staying here with him, they flew out the window now.

"Can I offer you anything to eat, Ms. Porter? And what about Sienna? You'll need to let me know what foods she likes."

At the mention of food, Kayla went distinctly green around the gills. A stricken look passed over her face and her blue eyes sought him out, silently beseeching him for help. Sudden understanding dawned. He took Sienna from her arms and quickly handed her to the surprised housekeeper.

"Call Annabelle down to meet her charge," he said to Imelda quickly before taking Kayla's hand and leading her to a downstairs bathroom.

She barely had time to utter a brief thanks before

she began to dry heave. Not knowing what else to do, and reluctant to leave her when she was obviously in such distress, Van rinsed a small hand towel under the cold tap and wrung it out before lifting her hair from her neck and gently placing the towel against her skin. He then continued to hold her hair to one side while she knelt on the tiled floor. After what felt like forever, she appeared to settle down.

"Thank you," she said shakily as he helped her to her feet. "I'm sorry you had to see that."

"It's hardly the first time I've seen you throw up," he said, remembering all too vividly Kayla's first highly illegal and disastrous encounter with alcohol when she was still a teenager. He and Sienna had taken turns looking after her that night so she wouldn't get in trouble with her parents. "Is this what happened to make you late on the way down, too?" he asked.

It was deeply concerning to realize she'd probably been driving while feeling so ill. It couldn't have been good for her concentration, let alone her and Sienna's safety.

"I didn't expect it to be so bad today. Honestly, it's been getting better, but..." Her voice trailed off.

"Kayla, really, you need to learn to accept help. It's clear you can't manage on your own. At least not until this has passed." If it passed, he reminded himself. The literature he'd read on the subject said some women struggled with hyperemesis gravidarum their entire pregnancy. Even beyond it.

"Well, you've seen to it that I don't have a choice

in that now, haven't you," she snapped. She sighed again and shook her head. "I'm sorry, Van. I'm being evil today. This situation…it just makes me feel as if I've lost all say in my own life."

He studied her. This was the most honest she'd been with him since breezing into his office a couple of months ago and dropping her bombshell into his carefully ordered world.

"This affects me, too, Kayla," he said gently. "I appreciate it's caused the most upheaval for you, and I am sorry about that, but you can't do this alone."

"I managed okay last time."

"You weren't caring for an almost one-year-old at the same time, though. Cut yourself some slack. For Sienna's sake if not for your own. Look, I'll show you to your room—you can have a nap secure in the knowledge that Sienna is being well cared for. When you're up to it, come down and have something light to eat."

He could see she wanted to fight him on his suggestion but exhaustion obviously won out.

"Fine, take me to my dungeon," she said with a theatrical sigh.

He arched one brow at her. "Dungeon? Really? That's what you think of me? Like I'm your jailer?"

She remained silent.

"Never mind," he muttered. "Come this way. You have your own en suite bathroom, so you'll have privacy if you're feeling unwell again. If you need help, though, you can dial one on your house phone and it'll connect you to Imelda straightaway."

"And Sienna?"

"Will be competently cared for by my staff. I'll check on her again after I've been in touch with my office. Don't worry—she'll be fine."

Kayla wanted to disagree. Putting Sienna in day care had been one thing, but now that she wasn't working, *she* wanted to be the one seeing to Sienna's needs. Even so, she felt so wrung out right now that if she didn't lie down soon, she'd probably fall down. And Van had already seen her brought low enough. It really would just be simpler, while she still fought the insidious nausea that lingered no matter how many times she was sick, to give in for now.

She followed him through the house to the main stairs and noticed that he slowed his pace to match her more lethargic gait. He'd been like that as a boy, too. Whenever her shorter legs couldn't keep up with him and Sienna as they'd headed off for an adventure together, he'd always slow and allow her to catch up. Of course, he'd never missed an opportunity to tease her about it. Even so, the memory was bittersweet. Back then, neither of them would ever have imagined they'd be where they were right now.

Determined not to give in to the hormones that threatened to bring tears to her eyes at the memory, she blinked furiously and almost bumped into Van's back when he stopped at a doorway.

"This is your room. You should find everything you need here. The bathroom is through there." He gestured to one side.

"Some dungeon," Kayla commented with a wan smile as she walked over to the open French doors and private balcony.

Gauzy sheer curtains drifted in the ocean breeze, making the room look like something out of a movie set. A king-size bed was positioned so the first thing she'd see each morning was the view out over the sea. Everything was tasteful and elegant with clean and simple lines and yet it still managed to be welcoming at the same time.

Van remained just inside the door, a strange expression on his face. "You're not a prisoner here, Kayla. You can come and go as you please."

Yes, she thought as she bent her head in acknowledgment, and also no. She might not have been a prisoner, but he still most definitely controlled her life. Now and for the foreseeable future. And no matter how beautiful her cage, she didn't like it one bit.

Seven

Kayla woke to find a small bottle of club soda and a plate with a few crackers on it on the bedside table. She felt embarrassed that someone had obviously come in and found her sleeping. Not only sleeping, but sleeping so deeply she hadn't even heard the person enter.

Her mouth was dry, so she took a sip of the soda and sat back on her pillows, relieved when it stayed down. After a few minutes, she swung her feet to the floor and slowly rose and moved over to the open French doors. Below, she caught the glimmer of sunlight on the water of a pool. She wondered where Sienna was and who had her, but she didn't have to wonder for long. On the grassy area near the pool, she saw a tall, leggy brunette bent over Sienna, holding her hands and helping her to walk. *That* was Annabelle? The woman looked too young to have the kind of experience that Van had alluded to, or maybe her experience came in other areas, as well?

Kayla forced herself to change the direction of her thoughts, putting them down to the fact that she just felt so uprooted. She'd never been the jealous type and she wasn't going to start now. And certainly not over Van.

It was weird. She'd spent the better part of her adult life traveling and experiencing new things. Until she'd lost her sister, it wouldn't have bothered her in the least to have had to move to a luxury home for a visit. The thing was, she'd grown used to the apartment she'd had in Lakeshore. It had become home from the second she'd brought Sienna back from the hospital. She'd worked hard to afford it, to make the money to pay the rent and put food on the table. It had been hers—she'd earned it. This place, though? It felt as if she was living inside someone else's dream.

That said, none of it was the nanny's fault, she reminded herself. It was childish to form a dislike for someone she'd never met based purely on a glimpse of them in a garden while they were doing their job. The fact that Van approved of her was also no reason to dislike the other woman even if she did seem to be particularly gifted when it came to grace and good looks. From the grass, Sienna gurgled and laughed, the sound bringing a faint smile to Kayla's face.

Her smile quickly died, though, when she saw Van join them and reach for Sienna. The baby went happily into her father's arms. The nanny touched Van's arm with a lingering hand, the caress surprising Kayla and making her wonder just how long he'd known Annabelle before installing her in the house to assist in Sienna's care. And hadn't he been on the verge of getting engaged to some other woman? Dani something-or-other? It seemed women came out of the woodwork to hang on his arm, Kayla thought sourly. Sienna, of course, was oblivious to the interplay of the two adults with her. Never one to be overly shy of strangers, Sienna settled easily with Van and didn't appear to be missing her mother at all. Watching the trio, Kayla felt again as though she was completely superfluous.

Van chose that exact moment to look up and he waved to Kayla and called out. "Are you feeling a little better? Come down and meet Annabelle."

Embarrassed at being caught spying on them, Kayla gave him a brief wave in response and rushed to her bathroom to freshen up. A few minutes later, showered, dressed in clothes that were less travel stained and with her hair brushed and pulled back in a ponytail, she made her way downstairs, wondering how to find her way to the lower terraced level where the pool was. Imelda bustled out from the kitchen and gave Kayla a smile and an approving nod when she saw Kayla carried the bottle of club soda.

"Mr. Murphy said for you to go down and meet them by the pool. I'll show you the way."

"Thank you," Kayla said with a smile in return. "And thank you for the snack and the soda water, too."

"Mr. Murphy asked me to leave it with you. He's very concerned for your health, and the baby's, too."

Imelda's words should have given Kayla some comfort but they made her feel more as if she was being managed—as if she was incapable of looking after herself. The housekeeper gave her a reassuring pat on the arm.

"Don't let him overwhelm you. He's just scared and isn't used to feeling that way—not to mention not being able to control what's happening. You and little Sienna are going to be good for him."

"Good for him? How?" Kayla blurted the question before stopping to think about it.

"He's locked himself up emotionally—I'm guessing that's something he taught himself to do a long time ago. It's why his engagement to Ms. Matthews worried both Jacob and me. He didn't need someone like her. He's a man who needs warmth and care. Like a plant that requires gentle coaxing and nurturing."

Kayla frowned. Nurturing? Van?

"Oh, and listen to me. Bombarding you with conversation when you probably just want to check on your wee girl. Follow me."

Imelda turned and led the way to another staircase that stretched to a lower level of the house. Kayla noted the mostly open-plan layout of the downstairs section, with its gaming room complete with full-size pool table, what looked like a home theater and, from what she spied through an open door, a guest suite, as well. Kayla followed Imelda out onto a patio and saw Van and Sienna playing on the grass, Annabelle standing to one side and watching.

"Before I go, let me know what you'd like the little one to have for dinner and what time you'd like her to eat."

Kayla gave Imelda a list of foods that Sienna ate and what to avoid. Imelda took it all on board.

"I'll get onto it now, then. See you up in the kitchen later, perhaps? Or would you prefer to eat on the balcony outside, where you won't have to deal with too many different aromas?"

"The balcony, please. Just for today."

"Not a problem. Ah, it looks like Sienna has spied her mama," Imelda commented with an indulgent smile.

Sure enough, Sienna, who by the look of things had been rolling on the grass with her father, was now crawling at high speed across the manicured lawn. Kayla quickly moved forward and bent to swoop her baby girl up in her arms, relishing the feel of Sienna's little body pressed against hers and the sensation of rightness now that she held her again. Van followed close behind.

"The rest has done you good," he commented. "You look more like your old self."

"I feel much better now, too." She decided to take the lead when it came to Annabelle and stepped toward her, holding out her hand. "Hi, I'm Kayla Porter, Sienna's mom."

Annabelle smiled and shook her hand. "You have

a beautiful daughter. I'm Annabelle Sorensen, but please call me Belle. Annabelle is such a mouthful."

The woman's smile was warm and friendly and Kayla felt something inside her ease. Apparently she'd been overreacting when she'd looked at them all before. Annabelle's manner was nothing but professional.

"Belle," Kayla repeated. "Good to meet you. I'm sorry I wasn't available earlier."

"No problem, Ms. Porter. My sister went through exactly the same thing with each of her pregnancies. I fully understand. You just tell me what you prefer for Sienna's routine and I'll do my best to ensure she's disrupted as little as possible during your time here."

And there it was. The reminder, unintentional or deliberate, that her time here was temporary. Kayla felt her smile stiffen but forced herself to relax. She had to be reading too much into Belle's statement. It seemed that being around Van was bringing out a defensive side of her that she didn't like. One that was as prickly as a desert cactus. She didn't like that person, she decided, and she was the only one who could change it.

Belle was looking at her, obviously awaiting a reply. Kayla summoned her best smile. Forget her antipathy toward Van; forget the obvious connection she'd witnessed between Van and Belle. She was going to play nice. Really nice.

"Thank you. I know it's just a job for you but I really appreciate it."

Okay, maybe not so nice, but she hadn't meant

that to come out quite the way it did. Even Van shot her a startled look.

Belle was all grace and charm in response. "I know exactly what you mean. Seriously, though, I'm not here to undermine you—only to help when you need it."

There was a genuineness in the woman's voice that made Kayla feel about two feet high. Van's cell phone chimed in his pocket and he checked the screen.

"Sorry, ladies, something I have to deal with straightaway. I'll leave you to get better acquainted."

He gave them each a brief smile and put the phone to his ear. Kayla caught him saying Dani's name as he strode away toward the house. So, despite what he'd said, they were still an item? Where did that leave the beautiful Belle? More important, where did that leave her? She shifted uncomfortably, not at all happy with where her thoughts were going.

"Are you okay? Would you like me to take Sienna for you?" Belle offered.

"I'm fine, thanks."

"She has a lovely name. Van tells me it was your sister's name, is that right?"

Belle was trying hard to make conversation and Kayla forced herself to be polite.

"Yes, Sienna is her child, actually."

"Van told me. I think it's a truly wonderful thing you're doing, having your sister's children."

"Van told you? That's rather personal information to share." Kayla couldn't keep the surprise or censure from her voice. They sure must have some boss-nanny relationship if he was getting down to nitty-gritty details like biological parents.

"Oh, Van and I go way back."

Kayla just stared at the nanny, her brain working overtime. Belle looked taken aback by her expression for a moment, but then she laughed.

"Oh, no. Not like that." She shook her head and laughed again. "Really nothing like that at all. Van served with my brother. After Nicholas died, Van took it upon himself to keep an eye out for our whole family. When he heard I was taking a break from pediatric nursing, he asked me if I would be interested in taking this job on. I jumped at the chance. I mean, look at this place—who wouldn't want to live here? Even my partner is jealous. She told me not to get ideas above my station."

Kayla didn't miss the reference to Belle's partner being female. She felt herself loosen up incrementally. Not that it made any difference. She had no say in who Van shared romantic interests with anyway. So why did she feel so stupidly relieved?

Kayla woke the next morning to a gentle knock at her bedroom door, followed by the sound of a high-pitched squeal and much splashing outside at the pool. She looked at the clock and realized, with a shock, that she'd slept through the night and past Sienna's usual waking time.

"Who is it?" she called.

"It's Imelda, dear. I've brought you a light breakfast."

Imelda came in through the door, balancing a tray on one arm.

Kayla sat up in bed feeling embarrassed. "Oh, I don't expect you to wait on me."

"Mr. Murphy's orders. You're to be coddled and cared for."

"He said that?"

"Well, not in those words exactly," Imelda said with a wink. "But he's insistent that you have nothing to worry about and that you're to get your rest."

"I really need to see to Sienna," Kayla protested as the housekeeper gently steered her back to her bed.

"All taken care of. Belle brought her down for breakfast at six thirty and now she's got her out by the pool with Mr. Murphy and Alex."

Alex, Van's Little Brother. Kayla remembered he was visiting today. She was curious about how the two interacted. While Van seemed intrigued by Sienna, seeing his interaction with the older child might give her some ideas as to what kind of father he planned to be. The news that Sienna was already down there with her father and Belle triggered Kayla's maternal instinct.

"Sienna's sunscreen, it was in the side pocket of—"

"Her diaper bag. Don't worry—Belle is on it. Now, you sit back in bed and enjoy your breakfast and take your time coming down. Today is going to be a good day, yes?"

"Well, so far, so good," Kayla admitted.

She sat back on the bed and Imelda positioned the tray over her thighs before removing the cover. Neat sections of dry toast were arranged on a plate along with a small bowl of sliced fruit. Imelda poured from a small teapot into a delicate china cup.

"The tea is lemon and ginger. Please tell me if it's not to your taste and we'll find something that is."

Kayla lifted the cup to her face and cautiously inhaled. "That smells good."

Imelda smiled. "Excellent. I'll be sure to tell Mr. Murphy that his research paid off. Now, he said you're to have small meals every two hours and we're going to work to keep your fluids up, as well."

"Goodness. That makes me feel so indulged," Kayla said with a laugh that failed to conceal her irritation.

"I know it seems a bit over the top, but Mr. Murphy was deeply concerned for you when you arrived yesterday. He really only wants what's best for you and the baby."

And that was where his care began and ended, Kayla was certain—with the baby. She was just the carrier. She felt like little more than a commodity. She took a wary sip of the tea and waited for the familiar surge of nausea that usually accompanied anything by mouth at this time of day, but thankfully, her stomach decided to accept the new introduction.

"Everything okay?" Imelda asked, hovering at the edge of the bed.

"Thank you—that really is lovely."

Imelda gave her a satisfied smile. "Good. We'll see you downstairs in a bit, then?"

"Definitely."

* * *

Van knew the instant that Kayla arrived down-stairs. That all-too-familiar awareness stroked the back of his neck even as Alex did his best to dunk him.

"Hold on a minute, Alex. We have a visitor."

He swam to the edge of the pool and pulled himself out of the water. Kayla approached from the house and made a beeline for Belle and Sienna, who were playing in a sheltered spot on the edge of the lawn. He searched her face for signs of the illness that had left her so run-down yesterday. He was relieved to see that Imelda's assessment of her health today had been correct. There was a faint blush of color in her cheeks and the shadows that had scored under her eyes yesterday were far less noticeable. Her skin still held a translucent quality, though—a fragility that he'd never associated with Kayla in the past. It spoke to him on a level that he was unaccustomed to these days, and the urge to protect her, and the child she carried, came stronger than he'd expected.

"Kayla," he said to acknowledge her approach. "I trust you slept well."

Her eyes flicked over his wet torso before settling back on his face, as if she was uncomfortable with his near nakedness.

"Very well, thank you. Is this Alex?" she asked, looking beyond him to the boy who'd just come from the pool to join him.

"Yes, hi," the twelve-year-old said, offering his hand as Van had taught him. "I'm Van's Little Brother."

"Pleased to meet you," Kayla said, taking the boy's

dripping-wet hand and shaking it. "I remember Van from when he was younger than you."

"Really? That's cool," the boy said exuberantly. "And you're still friends?"

Alex blushed as he realized the implication of what he'd just said.

"I'm sorry—" he started.

Kayla laughed and the sound was sweet and light and fresh. Everything he generally was not, Van thought. She always had been lightness to his dark. Sienna had fallen somewhere in between. The balancing rod that held them apart but kept them on an even keel at the same time.

"Nothing to be sorry about. I ask myself the same question," she said with a sharp look in Van's direction. "He was actually best friends with my sister, but, yeah, I guess we're still friends now."

"*Best* friends with a girl?" Alex gave Van a playful punch on the arm.

"A real guy can have girls for friends," Van retaliated.

"So where's your sister now?" Alex asked, giving Kayla his full attention again.

Van felt his gut clench and waited for Kayla's reply. She kept it brief.

"She died about five years back."

The boy looked uncomfortable, as if he'd just opened a can of worms he had no idea of how to deal with.

"Man, I'm sorry," he said with all the awkwardness of youth.

"Thank you," Kayla answered simply before smoothly changing the subject. "So, how long have you and Van been Brothers?"

Van watched as she captivated the boy—asking him questions, sharing a little of herself. She was natural with kids, he realized. She was already forming a friendship with Alex that had come a lot more quickly than his.

"And you're Sienna's mom?" Alex asked, his natural curiosity ignorant of the undercurrent that ran between Kayla and Van.

"Yes, that's right."

"How come she has a nanny, too?"

"Alex, remember we talked about this," Van interrupted. "Kayla hasn't been well and Belle is helping out."

"But Sienna is your baby, too, right? How does that work? Are you two together?"

Van thought about it carefully and settled on the clearest explanation he could come up with. "It's complicated."

"Why?"

He stifled a groan. He'd always encouraged Alex to ask questions—to delve deeper than the surface—in whatever he tackled. But this? How did you explain the situation to a twelve-year-old who was increasingly inquisitive about life? More important, how would he explain it in terms that wouldn't result in a call from Alex's mom tonight demanding to know what he was exposing her boy to? To his great relief, Kayla took over.

"Like Van said, it's complicated. Sienna always wanted kids, but she got sick and couldn't have them anymore. So I'm having them for her."

"Even though she's not alive anymore?"

"That's right."

Alex shrugged. "Sounds cool."

Van felt a surge of gratitude toward her for knowing exactly how much to say. No doubt he would have grossed Alex out with a far-too-detailed explanation.

The boy gave Van a cheeky grin and a light shove. "Last one in buys ice-cream sundaes in Carmel on the way home!" he yelled and took off back to the pool.

"Cheat!" Van answered with a laugh. "And no running beside the pool!" He turned to Kayla. "Thanks for that. He's a good kid, but he asks a lot of questions."

"No problem. You better go and join him. It's already going to cost you an ice-cream sundae. Who knows what else he'll add on if you take any longer?"

She gave him a smile that did strange things to his insides. He clamped down on the sensation. He didn't want to feel like that about Kayla. Not again. Attraction between them was a bad idea. They were polar opposites, for a start. Recognizing that he was beginning to try to rationalize his reactions, he decided it was a good time to go and join Alex. But as he started toward the pool again, he hesitated and turned toward her.

"You're welcome to come in, too. Bring Sienna in, if you like."

Oh, good one, Van, he silently growled. Like seeing her in an almost transparent muslin blouse and jeans wasn't doing stupid things to him already, he now wanted to see her in a bikini? He was certifiably nuts. She wouldn't accept. She'd made it pretty clear she wanted to be around him little more than he wanted to be in her vicinity.

Kayla appeared to consider his question. "It's still a little cold out, isn't it?"

"I can wait at the edge with a towel to wrap Sienna in the second she's ready to come out," Belle suggested from behind Kayla. "Really, the pool is lovely. Van keeps it temperature controlled all year round."

Kayla gave a brief nod. "Okay. She'd like that. She's been a water baby right from the start. Just give me about ten minutes to get her ready, okay?"

"And you? Will you be coming in, too?" Van couldn't help asking. Maybe she'd refuse.

For a second he thought she was going to, but then she gave him another nod. "Sure."

"Okay. I'll wear some of the energy off this guy in the meantime," Van said.

He watched as she walked toward Belle, who was sitting in the shade with Sienna, and felt that uncomfortable pull in his chest again. Damn, why had he done that? He'd invited her here to his home so she could stay well while pregnant with his child. Just at the reminder that Kayla carried *his child*, the pull intensified and a rush of possessiveness swept through him.

"Damn," he muttered under his breath. No matter what he said, no matter what he did, he still wanted her. He deliberately turned his back and jogged toward the pool. Wanting her was one thing, he reminded himself. But having her was a complication he wasn't going near again—ever.

Eight

What on earth had she been thinking? Kayla asked herself as she carried Sienna upstairs to her nursery to change her into swim diapers and her little UV-protection sunsuit. She didn't want to spend any more time with Van than absolutely necessary and yet she had just agreed to do so—and swimming, no less.

For a moment she remembered how fine he'd looked coming out of the pool. His tanned skin glistening with water. Droplets caressing the contours of his body. Kayla felt her body react to the memory. Felt her heart rate increase and a flush of heat bloom deep inside. Well, at least it wasn't nausea, she told herself in an attempt to drag her attention away from just how very attractive he'd looked.

She should simply bring Sienna down ready for

the water and forego a swim herself. But the lure of the pool with its temperature control was too strong. She loved the water. Loved the weightless feeling of floating. Besides, how much trouble could she get herself into when chaperoned by an eleven-month-old baby and a boy of twelve?

Even so, as she changed into her bikini, she began to reassess the wisdom of her decision. Her breasts were already fuller than normal and filled the cups of her halter-neck top and then some. This certainly wasn't appropriate wear in front of a couple of kids, she decided while checking her reflection in the mirror. She grabbed a thin T-shirt and pulled it on over the top. There, that was better. It also hid the slight bump that she was beginning to develop. She'd started to show so much earlier with this pregnancy, particularly with the weight loss she'd endured so far.

On the floor at her feet, Sienna looked a picture in her ruffled pink-and-white sunsuit.

"Aren't you just the cutest thing," she said, gathering her daughter up in her arms. "Your mommy would have loved you so much."

A wave of melancholy washed through her but she fought it back. Darn hormones were sending her emotions all over the place. But it felt good to remember Sienna, to think of how happy her sister would be to see her baby well cared for in such a beautiful place. She had to remember that she was living her dream of honoring her sister's wish—and not alone. Van was participating, too, albeit in a rather draconian way. She had to believe that things would work out the best for the children, and she had to hold on to that thought no matter what crazy ideas came into her head about Van.

Alex was out of the pool when she returned downstairs but Van remained in the water, now swimming strong laps back and forth. Some sixth sense must have warned him she'd returned because she had only just drawn close to the stairs when he stopped and swam toward her.

"Pass her to me," he said. "I'll play with her while you relax."

She was about to point out that she was perfectly capable of playing with her own daughter in the water but bit back the words that automatically sprang to her lips. She had felt a pang of envy when she'd seen Van swimming. It had been a while since she'd been able to do anything but paddle in the water with Sienna.

"Thanks," she said, handing a gleeful kicking baby to her father.

Sienna instantly splashed the water, making Van laugh. The sound was rich and deep and Kayla felt her lips pull into an answering smile. She watched the two of them as Van held Sienna carefully and began floating backward, kicking his legs like a lazy frog. They looked so perfect together, father and child. He'd missed so much of Sienna's development to date but he seemed resolved toward making the most of his time with her now. And there she went again with the waterworks springing to her eyes.

It had been her decision not to tell Van that she was having his children, even though she'd known her sister wouldn't have approved. His initial response to her a couple of months ago had made her glad she hadn't contacted him sooner, but seeing him with Sienna now was making her a little regretful on his behalf. Of course, back then, she hadn't known how he felt about having kids, but now that he had them…? Well, he certainly seemed to be adapting quickly.

If only she didn't still get this buzz of attraction simmering under her skin whenever she was around him. It made life difficult, to say the least. Did he feel the same thing, she wondered, that hint of physical memory of the passion they'd lost themselves in? Probably not. After all, if he had, he wouldn't have left without any further contact, would he? She had to remind herself of that. Had to hold on to the disappointment and anger she'd felt when she'd woken up alone after falling asleep in his arms. And hope like heck that he'd changed and that he wouldn't be a deserter when it came to his kids.

Kayla lowered herself into the pool, enjoying the texture of the water against her skin as she swam. The T-shirt she'd put on felt a little restrictive, though, as she did slow laps. She'd have to see if she could find a one-piece swimsuit. One that would see her through at least part of her pregnancy, with any luck. After a couple of minutes, she rolled onto her back and allowed herself to float.

"Enjoying it?" Van asked from nearby.

"Very much."

"Make use of the pool as much as you like. Day or night."

"Thank you."

She put her feet to the pool floor and looked at Sienna, who was happily still splashing and being floated around by Van. His hands were big and capable as they tucked under Sienna's armpits and his fingers closed around her little back. She looked safe with him, and incredibly happy. At the edge of the pool, Belle waited—her long legs dangling in the water and a thick fluffy white towel in her hands.

"Do you think she's had enough, Kayla?" Belle asked. "I'm taking Alex inside for a prelunch snack and I can take Sienna in, too, if you like."

"He's hungry again?" Van laughed. "That kid, he never stops eating."

"I'm a growing boy," Alex interjected from the deck chair where he'd been playing a game on his phone under the shade of the house's overhang.

Van turned to Kayla. "Kayla? You happy for Sienna to go with Belle?"

"I can take her," she protested.

"No, it's okay," Belle said. "You stay and enjoy your swim. We'll just be upstairs in the kitchen when you're finished."

If she refused now, she'd only appear churlish, Kayla forced herself to admit. "Okay, thanks. I won't be much longer."

"Take all the time you want," Belle answered with a smile and got to her feet so she could wrap Sienna in the towel.

Van made motorboat noises as he pushed the baby through the water, making her squeal with delight, and again, Kayla felt herself smiling in response. This really was good for her little girl. There was only so much the teachers at day care could do and this interaction with other people was opening up her tiny world beyond what she'd known to date. Kayla felt a sudden shame that she hadn't stopped to consider that aspect of what Van had to offer Sienna before today. She'd done her very best to make sure that Sienna had everything she needed, always. But she had the sense now that maybe it hadn't been enough.

Not liking the direction of her thoughts, Kayla returned to swimming laps. She kept her pace slow and steady, not wanting to wear herself out too much. Tiredness always exacerbated her nausea. She'd been at it for about ten more minutes before she felt a firm touch on her shoulder midstroke.

"You always were like a fish in water," Van said from right beside her. "But I think it's time you stopped for today."

She couldn't help it. Her temper flared. "Van, can we come to some kind of agreement that you will stop telling me what to do all the time? I'm an adult. I'm capable of looking after myself quite adequately."

"That's true," he answered, giving her a level look. "But in this case, with my baby inside you, adequate is not good enough."

She stared at him, seeing the unyielding determination in his gaze. His eyes seemed an even deeper green than usual as he stared back at her—his lashes black spikes from the pool and his dark hair matted close to his skull. He'd always been the only person who could match her in the water when they were kids and she realized that even back then, while he'd kept an emotional distance from her—trusting only her sister with his most personal secrets—he'd never physically been far away.

The thing was, when he'd been close before, she'd never felt the urge to place her hand on his bare chest the way she did now. Never wanted to trace the definition of his pectoral muscles or to run her fingers over the clearly defined six-pack of his abdomen. Or even to run the tip of her tongue along the cords of his neck and the line of his jaw.

She tried to focus on what he'd said. To draw her irritation to the surface, to use it to quench the slow-burning desire that had lit inside her, but it was useless. It seemed that, once lit, this fire couldn't be extinguished.

"Ms. Porter? It's time for your snack," Imelda called from the patio. The tension between them broke. Van took a step back and mustered up a false-looking half smile.

"See? Even Imelda thinks it's time you got out of the pool."

"Imelda is only doing what you tell her to do," Kayla muttered, annoyed with herself as much as she was with him.

But she didn't argue. Instead she swam to the edge of the pool and lifted herself out. Her T-shirt sucked onto her body like a second skin. Wet and now see-through as a result, it afforded her no protection from Van's gaze. She stood and grabbed the hem of the gar-

FREE Merchandise is 'in the Cards' for you!

Dear Reader,

We're giving away FREE MERCHANDISE!

Seriously, we'd like to reward you for reading this novel by giving you **FREE MERCHANDISE** worth over $20 retail. And no purchase is necessary!

You see the Jack of Hearts sticker above? Paste that sticker in the box on the Free Merchandise Voucher inside. Return the Voucher today... and we'll send you Free Merchandise!

Thanks again for reading one of our novels—and enjoy your Free Merchandise with our compliments!

Pam Powers

Pam Powers

P.S. Look inside to see what Free Merchandise is **"in the cards"** for you!

BUSINESS REPLY MAIL
FIRST-CLASS MAIL   PERMIT NO. 717   BUFFALO, NY

POSTAGE WILL BE PAID BY ADDRESSEE

READER SERVICE
PO BOX 1867
BUFFALO NY 14240-9952

NO POSTAGE
NECESSARY
IF MAILED
IN THE
UNITED STATES

ment, twisting and wringing it to try to get rid of the excess moisture and to pull it away from her body. Van watched her the whole time, his eyes traveling over the prominent swell of her breasts and lower to the tiny bump of her belly.

Color appeared along his cheekbones, and his jaw firmed as though he clenched his teeth. Feeling uncomfortable under his stare, Kayla turned her back and walked to where Imelda had set a small tray on a table under a sun umbrella. Even so, she felt him continue to watch her.

Imelda picked up a robe off the back of the chair. "Here—you should take that shirt off and wrap yourself up in this before you get cold. It's not quite summer yet," she chided gently.

"Oh, that's not mine—" Kayla corrected.

"No, it's mine," Van said from behind her.

Kayla jumped. She hadn't heard him approach. He stood behind her, swiping his body with a large towel, which he then casually wrapped around his hips.

"But please, put it on," he continued.

Feeling awkward and already cold from the breeze that came in off the sea, Kayla peeled the shirt off and dropped it on the patio with a wet slap. Van had taken the robe from Imelda and held it out for her. The second the thick toweling wrapped around her, she felt warmer, but no less uncomfortable as a faint trace of Van's scent enveloped her.

"What about you? W-won't you get c-cold?" she stammered.

"I'm okay for now. Will it bother you if I have coffee with you here? I promise to stay downwind."

"Bother me? No, I don't think so." The aroma of coffee might not bother her right at this moment, but he most certainly did. "But shouldn't you be with Alex?"

"He'll be okay for now, won't he, Imelda?"

"He's gone with Jacob for now, Mr. Murphy. They're stacking the flat rocks together for the water feature in the front garden. He's a very tactile child, isn't he?"

Van smiled, the brief flash of good humor sending a jolt of awareness through Kayla as if it was a lover's touch.

"That's one way of saying he wants to keep his fingers in as many pies as possible. Let Jacob know he's to send Alex to me if he's any bother."

Imelda smiled indulgently. "Oh, he's no bother. Jacob enjoys his company." She turned to Kayla. "Belle is putting Sienna down for a nap. She seemed a bit tired after her time in the pool. Belle said to tell you."

Kayla nodded. "That's good. She normally sleeps for an hour or so before lunch anyway."

Van raised a brow at her.

"What?" she demanded as Imelda returned upstairs.

"No dispute or argument at Belle's high-handedness?"

She took his teasing lightly. "No. She's merely following routine."

"And you have an hour or so to rest," he pointed out. "Is the food to your liking?"

Kayla looked at the plate of neatly cut raw vegetables and chose a slice of carrot to nibble on. "Tastes fine. Thank you, but I don't need to rest."

A frown of concern pulled between his brows.

"Don't bully me, Van," she interrupted before he could speak.

Van looked at her in surprise. "Bully you? Is that how you see it?"

"Tell me how else I should see it," she said. "You keep telling me what to do."

Her tone implied she was struggling to keep a grip on her temper. He'd never known her to be this fiery. She'd always had a sunny, easygoing nature. But then, he guessed a lot had changed since he'd known her truly well. And he'd never known her pregnant.

He looked at her. Dressed in his robe, she looked tiny, swamped, even. But when she'd gotten out of the pool just now, he hadn't missed the fullness of her breasts or the intriguing shape of her lower belly. If he hadn't already known how taut her body normally was, he probably wouldn't have thought much of it, but he couldn't help feeling that twinge of pride and possession when he'd considered that his child was nestled there.

It was strange and terrifying at the same time. He couldn't help wondering—had he unwittingly passed on the genetic predisposition of his family to his children? He wasn't certain he'd avoided it himself. He'd cut alcohol completely from his life—but was that enough? Even if he never took a drink again, the craving for it was still written in his DNA. It could still be inherited by his children.

He looked at Kayla's face and realized she was still waiting for his response. He scrambled to remember exactly what it was she'd said. Something about bullying.

"Perhaps, Kayla, it's more about caring. Have you ever considered that?"

He reached for the thermos coffee carafe Imelda had left on the table for him and poured the dark brew into his mug.

"Don't lie to me, Van. We both know you don't care about me. And I'm fine with that. Let's just agree to be honest with each other."

She shifted in her chair and the front of his robe opened, exposing the curves of her breasts and the shadowy valley between. Hell, he'd seen more of her when she was dressed in that clinging wet shirt than he did now and yet somehow this glimpse of her in his robe sent a punch of lust through his body that made his hand shake as he set the carafe back on the table.

"I'm all for being honest," he said, staring straight into her blue eyes. "Tell me, why does staying here chafe you so much?"

"I'm not used to being so—" she paused, her brow furrowing as she searched for the right word "—coddled."

"What, like an egg?" he teased, making himself keep his tone light.

"For want of a better analogy, yes. Except I'm the one coddling an egg, aren't I?"

He laughed. "Kind of. You know you can come

and go as you please. Like I said yesterday, you're not a prisoner here."

"And Sienna? I can take her with me as I come and go as I please?"

He hesitated and it was enough to ignite the fuse on her anger.

"See? That's exactly what I'm talking about. I'm her mother, for goodness' sake! I carried her, I birthed her, I've been her primary carer from the day she arrived in this world. Me. Not some overpaid nanny. Not some man who suddenly wants to control every aspect about the children he stopped caring about before they were even born!"

"I care," he said softly, lethally. "Don't ever underestimate that, Kayla."

"No, controlling everything around you is not caring. It's smothering. Really, Van, you need a reality check."

"And I guess you think you're the person to give it to me?" he snapped back.

"I wouldn't even bother," she sniffed.

The gentle breeze swirled around them and he noticed that Kayla had suddenly blanched.

"Are you okay?" he asked, setting his mug down on the table.

"Oh, please. Enough with the concern. I just got a whiff of your coffee. Neither it nor your company agrees with me. If you'll excuse me, I'm going inside."

She pushed her seat back sharply and rose from the table. The neckline of the robe gaped again, and damned if he didn't get that powerful burst of arousal once more.

Despite the fighting, despite their obvious frustration with one another, his body and his brain were completely out of sync. He rose, too, putting a hand out to stop her. She stared at his fingers curled over the white toweling that encased her arm, then up at his face.

"If you don't want me to throw up on your feet, I'd advise you to let me go," she said in a voice that hinted that she was barely holding on to her control.

He let his hand drop and watched as she made her way back inside. What the hell was wrong with him? And why did she bring out the worst in him even now that he was a man grown and fully in charge of his senses? Well, fully in charge when he wasn't around her, at least.

"Van, Van! Come and see what we made!" Alex came dashing around the side of the house, dancing with excitement.

"I'm on my way," Van answered, grateful for the distraction.

And that was something Kayla Porter had always been. A distraction through and through. Maybe it hadn't been such a great idea bringing her here, but if he wanted a place in his children's lives, he had to accept she was part of the deal. For now, at least.

It didn't mean he didn't want to throttle her every now and then, though. Throttle her or something else? A tiny voice at the back of his mind poked at him, reminding him of his reaction to her just now. No, he wasn't going there, he thought. Not again. Because he knew that if he did, he'd never be able to walk away like he had the last time.

Nine

After her altercation with Van, Kayla worked hard to steer clear of him over the next few days. It wasn't too difficult. Early each morning, he drove to the Monterey Airport and piloted his helicopter to work in San Francisco. And he put in long hours. Whether that was all work and no play was none of her business, she reminded herself firmly as she looked at the clock in the main entrance on her way upstairs. So what if it was nine thirty and he was still nowhere to be seen? However, for a man who'd said he wanted to have more to do with his children, he was doing a mighty poor job of spending time with his daughter.

And there she was again. Annoyed at him. Angry. Neither of which were her natural state. She'd always been sunny natured. Cheerful. Able to look on the bright side of pretty much everything all the time. But living under the same, albeit expansive, roof as Van Murphy was totally doing her head in. The last few nights, she'd resumed doing a little yoga before bed. It helped her to center herself and she certainly needed centering right now.

Since she was already dressed in a loose-fitting pair of stretch pants and one of her favorite tie-dyed shirts, she walked across to the large square of carpet in the living room and slipped off her shoes. The fibers of the carpet were thick and spongy beneath her bare feet and she wriggled her toes in them, enjoying the sensation against her skin. When was the last time she'd taken a minute just to be in the moment? Sure, she'd been doing her exercises but more as a matter of rote, not so much as a state of mind.

She lowered into a deep squat, lifted her arms and pressed her palms together in front of her as though in prayer, then closed her eyes and consciously made an effort to relax. Slowly, she breathed in and out, clearing her mind of thoughts.

It lasted all of about two minutes before her mind was racing ahead thinking about Van again. She was annoyed with him for spending so long away from home. Sienna might not know any better now, but it wouldn't be long before she got old enough to notice. Was this really the kind of father he intended to be—an absentee one?

But then she remembered watching him with Alex last Saturday. It had been quite an eye-opener. He was different with the boy than he was with her. Not as dictatorial, for a start, she noted with a huff of irritation.

Stop it, she told herself. *Stop thinking about him. Relax. Empty your mind. Breathe in. Breathe out.* She worked through her sun-salutation warm-up routine but the Big Brother version of Van continued to intrude.

She'd been intrigued by the man she'd seen. To encourage Alex to continue to strive hard, he'd even promised the kid a ride in his helicopter if he kept his grades up until the end of the school year. He was firm with the boy but kind about it. *Almost*, dare she say it, *nurturing*. It was interesting to reflect on, she thought as she moved into her first pose with an ease and familiarity from years of experience. Maybe he was offering Alex what he'd missed out on all those years as a child himself.

Heaven knew his parents were stricter than most. His family situation had been so very different from hers growing up. Her parents had always made a fuss over a good report, having a special meal at home or buying a small trinket of one kind or another. Every achievement was celebrated, while any failures were looked upon as an opportunity to learn and receive encouragement. Van's parents, not so much. If he failed a class, or even got a bad grade on a test or a paper, he'd get a beating. But he'd always brush the bruises and scrapes off as a result of being clumsy, never admitting what had really happened.

He'd spent a lot of time at her house. She could still see him sitting at the table of her parents' dining room, watching silently as her dad made a little speech when she'd won a creativity award in elementary school. He'd kept himself aloof, yet he was clearly yearning to be a part of the warmth that had made their family's house a home. Was that what he'd meant when he'd told her this was home for him? That he wanted to re-create the sense of belonging that her family had always taken for granted? It was a question to tuck away and ponder later, she decided.

Kayla began her standing asanas, finally feeling as though she was in the moment. She was balanced on one leg, her hand holding the tip of her left foot as she extended it out beside her.

"Is that safe?"

As if her thoughts had summoned him, there he was. Standing right behind her with yet another disapproving frown creasing between his brows. Kayla lowered her leg and planted both feet firmly on the ground.

"If it wasn't, do you think I'd be doing it?" she countered in as reasonable a tone as she could manage.

While part of her was strangely relieved to see him, another was frustrated that just as she'd managed to focus on her meditation, he'd come along and yanked her back out of it.

He looked tired. His tie had been pulled loose and the top two buttons of his pristine white shirt were undone, exposing the hollow at the base of his tanned throat. She'd kissed him there, she remembered before snapping her mind back out of the past.

"Is everything okay?" she asked.

"Yeah, just busy. We're ironing out glitches in a new system and it's the usual—whatever can go wrong will go wrong."

"Sounds like you could use a bit of yoga yourself." She smiled. "Or a stiff whiskey."

His face froze. "I don't drink."

"Oh, I didn't realize you'd given it up. Any particular reason?" she probed without thinking. "Oh, heck, that was probably a bit personal. I'm sorry. You don't have to answer that if you don't want to."

He gave her a cursory smile and ignored her question altogether. "Have you made plans for tomorrow?"

"Plans? No, not really. Sienna's cutting a tooth at the moment but if she's not too grouchy, I thought I could take her to the aquarium in Monterey. I considered the zoo, but, you know, too many smells."

She gave a self-deprecating laugh. The nausea was more manageable now that she was getting so much more rest, but she didn't think she was up to facing the various aromas to be encountered on a late spring morning at the zoo.

"Sounds like a good idea. Do you mind if I join you?"

Kayla couldn't hide her surprise. "Isn't tomorrow a business day for you?"

"One of the perks of being the boss. I can take time off when I want. But I don't have to, if you'd rather take her on your own."

Kayla was reminded of the aloof boy of her childhood. Always on the fringe. Never inserting himself where he feared he wasn't wanted. She made a decision.

"No. I mean, she'd love it if you came, too."

Van's eyes met hers, a flicker of something in their emerald depths. "And you?"

Her breath caught in her throat. It was hard to put a label on how she felt about deliberately spending time with him. "I'd appreciate the extra pair of hands with Sienna, of course."

The flicker of light she thought she'd seen reflected in his eyes dimmed a little. "Have you been feeling better this week?" he asked, moving into the sitting room and relaxing onto one of the deep chairs.

"Each day seems to get a little better."

He nodded in apparent approval. "That's good. And you haven't been overdoing things?"

Kayla sighed. "No, your troops have made sure I barely lifted a finger all week."

His mouth quirked into that sweet half smile that seemed like a kindness compared to his usually somber visage. "They had their orders. You're looking a lot better for the rest. What time were you thinking of heading out tomorrow?"

"They don't open until ten, and Imelda tells me it only takes about fifteen minutes or so from here."

"So, leave at oh-nine-forty-five?"

She fought the urge to salute him. "Sure, that sounds fine. But like I said, it'll depend on how grumpy Sienna is."

"With both of us to distract her, I'm sure we'll

manage." He stifled a yawn. "If you'll excuse me, I'll head up to bed."

A vision of him, naked against crisp white sheets, flooded her mind. Kayla felt a warm blush spread across her face. "Sleep well," she said, her voice suddenly more husky than normal.

Van looked back at her and for the briefest moment she thought she saw that flare in his eyes again— something primal and heated. Something that reminded her of the man she'd taken to bed five years ago. Kayla's mouth grew dry, every cell in her body attuned to his next move. But all too quickly that look was gone, leaving her wondering if she hadn't imagined it after all.

She stood there transfixed by her imagination as he left the room and headed up the main staircase. A tremor rippled through her. He was an attractive man; of course she'd have some kind of physical reaction to him, especially knowing what they'd been capable of together, but this felt like something more. Something she really didn't want to examine any further. Something that could become very messy emotionally if she allowed herself to think about it too much.

Hormones, she told herself. *You're just in crazy mode, where everything either drives you mad, makes you cry or...or turns you on*, whispered a little voice in the back of her mind. Kayla shook her head, as if the physical action could rid her of the reality she didn't want to admit. The truth that despite his deserting her after their one night together, despite the way he'd more recently run roughshod over her and taken control of her life, she still wanted him.

Wanted, yes. But having was another thing entirely and it so wasn't going to happen, she resolved sternly. Not only because she didn't want it to, but because he so clearly didn't, either. She wasn't about to set herself up for complete rejection again. It had been hard enough the last time. Now she was so much more vulnerable.

Kayla tried to resume her yoga routine but her mind simply wouldn't let go for long enough for anything to flow. Giving it up altogether, she switched off the lights and made her way to her room. Hours later she still couldn't get to sleep. Her mind kept offering alternative scenarios of where things could have gone with Van after he'd said good-night. Scenarios that left her feeling as though she had an itch somewhere that, no matter what, she simply couldn't relieve.

Van was up early the next morning and was surprised to find Kayla already downstairs with Sienna.

"Belle not up?" he said after wishing them a good morning.

He studiously tried to ignore the fact that Kayla was obviously still in her pajamas. The tank top clung to her full breasts and the bottoms hung low on her hips, exposing the slight roundness of her belly.

Kayla gave him a long-suffering look. "You can't expect the woman to have night duties with Sienna and then be up at the crack of dawn, as well. Besides, it's her day off today. You know, that time when normal people do normal things like, oh, I don't know—not work, maybe?"

He looked at her in surprise. "Did you get out on the wrong side of the bed this morning?"

"No, I did not and my morning has been perfectly lovely."

Until now. Even he could hear the unsaid words hanging in the air.

"Dadadadadad!"

Both adults turned to the baby in the high chair. Van felt a rush of elation thrill through him.

"What did she say?"

"You heard her. She's been saying it since she woke up this morning."

Ah, maybe that explained the bad mood, Van thought. He flashed a smile at Sienna, who reached out her arms toward him.

"You'll want to wipe her hands first," Kayla commented.

She rose from the kitchen table and moved toward the counter, where she rinsed a small muslin cloth under the tap before handing it to him. Van looked at her a moment before understanding. She expected him to wipe the baby's hands? That should be interesting, he thought. Aside from occasionally holding Sienna and playing with her in the pool the other day, he'd actually had very little to do with her. Right now a full-combat mission would have been less daunting.

"You'll get best results if you hold her lower forearm with one hand and then use your other with the cloth to clean her hand. And make sure you get between her fingers, too," Kayla advised.

She leaned against the counter and eyed him with a look that, if he hadn't known better, he'd have said was almost gleeful.

"What exactly is that muck she's got on her hands?"

"Mashed banana mostly."

"Mostly?"

"And some cereal. Sets pretty hard if you don't wash it out of your clothes or hair straightaway. Stains, too."

"Dadadadadad!" Sienna exclaimed cheerfully, suddenly putting her hands on her head and transferring a lot of the mess into her hair.

"Oh, hell, now what?" Van asked, instantly feeling utterly helpless.

Kayla chuckled. At first the sound was slight, as if it had slipped out despite her best attempts not to laugh, but then it grew and took shape until she was in paroxysms of laughter.

"Your face," she wheezed between bouts of uncontrolled laughing. "I wish you could see your face."

Van shifted uncomfortably. He'd survived the regular beatings his adoptive dad had given him. He'd spent the better part of ten years in the army seeing active service. He'd built a multimillion-dollar company from the ground up. He would not let this defeat him.

"C'mon, Sienna. Be a good girl for your daddy," he coaxed.

He moved forward carefully, holding the cloth as if it was some magic talisman or enchanted weapon.

"She's a baby, not a wild animal," Kayla observed. Another chuckle escaped her.

The baby laughed, too, and the sound of her full-bellied little laugh coaxed a similar response from Van.

"Maybe I should just take her outside and hose her," he said.

"Yeah, I know it's tempting but I don't think that's completely necessary. Go on, she won't bite. Or are you scared?"

Her last words hardened his resolve. He surged forward, took one little arm and wiped the hand as quickly as he could, then did the same with the other. Sienna, of course, immediately put her hands back in the slop in her bowl and applied them straight to her hair again. Behind him, Kayla exploded into laughter once more, generating even more baby giggles from Sienna.

"You know, you really shouldn't encourage her. These are not nice table manners," he said grimly.

He took the bowl from the high-chair tray and set it in the kitchen sink before rinsing off the cloth and approaching Sienna again—this time with a determination that he would not fail. She tugged her tiny hands as he cleaned them but he was firm as he gently wiped them. Then he did the best he could with her hair before unbuckling her harness and lifting her from the chair.

"How's that?" he said as he faced Kayla again, feeling ridiculously triumphant.

She nodded slowly and pursed her lips. "Not bad. Needs work, but not bad at all."

She took the cloth off him and rinsed it out before teasing Sienna with it while managing to remove the last of the goop from her hair. He watched in surprise at how adept she was.

"You're really good at that," he commented.

"I've had a few more months of practice."

It struck him how much she'd dealt with on her own for so long—and how well she'd coped. He'd never have thought it of her. She'd always been the one that got into trouble at school with her teachers—mostly for daydreaming and not turning in her homework or assignments on time. She'd eschewed attending college, instead choosing to take a year to indulge her wanderlust. A year that turned into several years as she traveled around the world. But she'd been there for her sister when crunch time came and Sienna really started to go downhill, he remembered. Which was a damn sight more than he'd been.

"I know I've never acknowledged this before, but you've done a really good job with Sienna," he said in all seriousness. "She's a beautiful baby. Thank you."

"Well, I didn't have her for your sake," Kayla responded tartly, but he could see the gleam of pleasure that glowed in her eyes at his words.

"I know that, but I'm grateful."

"Grateful that I didn't tell you that you were going to be a father?"

He absently pressed his lips to the top of his daughter's head and inhaled the lingering scents of banana, cereal and baby that mingled together.

"Yeah, I guess I am. I would have stopped you somehow and then…" He let his voice trail off.

"And then we wouldn't be here now," Kayla finished for him.

She turned away to rinse out Sienna's bowl and stack it in the dishwasher and he watched her, unmistakably drawn to the way the fabric of her pajama bottoms tightened around the curve of her bottom as she bent to insert the bowl. His body awakened in response and he tamped the sensation back. This was Kayla. The mother of the baby in his arms and now carrying another child he'd never expected to want or to love. He shouldn't feel this way about her. She straightened up and looked at him.

"What?" she demanded. "Have I ripped my pants or something?"

"No, no. Nothing like that."

"Are you okay with Sienna while I go and grab my shower? There's a stack of books in the box in the corner there," she said, gesturing to the more casual sitting room to the other side of the kitchen. "She likes to be read to."

"You're going to leave her alone…with me?"

"You're her father, aren't you? Being a dad is a bit more than cleaning her up once and taking her to the aquarium. You've been pretty scarce since we've been here. I thought you wanted to get to know your daughter," Kayla challenged him.

"I wanted to know she was safe and well cared for and that you were, too," he defended.

"But you didn't want to be hands-on?"

He hesitated. To be totally honest, he had no idea of how to be a good father. His birth parents had been deemed incapable of caring for him and at the age of three he'd been adopted by a couple who'd wanted to be parents but who'd had no idea of what it took to nurture a child. The only example of fatherhood he'd had was Kayla's own dad. He wondered if the man had ever felt as confused and cast adrift with his daughters as Van did right now.

"I don't know what I expected. But I do want to be a good father. I want to keep her safe, always."

Kayla's expression softened. "Van, you're not your father. You won't lift a hand to Sienna in anger. I know you're stronger than that. Is that what's bothering you? That you think you might turn into him?"

"He wasn't my father," Van shocked himself by answering. "I was adopted."

"You...you what? Adopted? Really? When did you find that out?"

"Not long after your sister died. I shouldn't have been surprised, really."

Kayla moved across the kitchen and put a hand on his arm. Her blue eyes reflected her concern for him. "It can't have been an easy discovery."

"It wasn't. It made me reassess things, though. And now I'm reassessing again."

He looked at the baby in his arms. A child that was a blend of both him and her biological mother. Could he do this? Could he be a good dad? Had he inadvertently passed on a potential death sentence to this beautiful sweet child?

Kayla moved a step back. He felt the loss of her touch instantly. "Every day is a new day, Van. You can start over as often as you like."

And that summed her up perfectly. Always starting over, always looking for the next adventure. He'd long considered her to be lacking in commitment, but the background search he'd ordered into her life showed that since her sister had passed away, she'd knuckled down, just like she'd said, and lived a stable lifestyle. With the exception of her providing a roof over the head of a series of homeless people, of course. But even then, she'd been trying to do something good. He understood that aside from the last incident, the people she'd helped had mostly gone on to better things and happier lives once they'd gotten onto their feet again. Maybe he needed to take a leaf out of her book for a change instead of trying to pigeonhole her where he thought she should fit.

The realization was sobering. Where exactly did he think she fitted? Right now he wanted her here to ensure that she didn't endanger the baby she was carrying or herself—let alone the child he now held in his arms. But what about after the new baby came along? Where did he want Kayla to fit then?

Ten

It was quiet when Kayla came back downstairs after her shower. She knew Imelda wouldn't be far away when she left the kitchen, so she wasn't too worried about leaving Van with Sienna, but she was surprised that neither of them were in the room where she'd left them twenty minutes ago. She found Imelda bustling around with her customary efficiency.

"Good morning, Ms. Porter," the housekeeper said cheerfully. "Looks like when the cloud burns off, it's going to be a beautiful day."

"Yes, it does." No matter how many times Kayla asked Imelda to use her first name, the woman insisted on the more formal address. "Have you seen Van and Sienna? I left them here when I went for my shower a little while ago."

Imelda beamed. "Oh, yes. They've gone into the garage. Jacob arrived with a new delivery for Mr. Murphy. He said for you to go through when you were down."

The garage? Kayla frowned. "Do you know what that's about?"

The housekeeper continued grinning. "Yes, I do, but don't ask me what it is, because it's meant to be a surprise. You go on through and find out."

There was nothing left to do but obey so Kayla followed the corridor that led toward the three-car garage and pushed open the connecting door. She stopped in her tracks when she saw what was there. Or, more to the point, what wasn't.

"Where's my car?" she asked, looking through the open garage door to the driveway to see if it had been moved.

"Right here," Van said, straightening from the backseat, where he'd been securing Sienna in a car seat, and gesturing to the gleaming Audi SUV parked where her car should have been.

"That's not my car, Van. This isn't funny. You said I wasn't a prisoner here but now you've taken my car away from me?"

"Kayla, relax. This *is* your car now." He took a set of keys from his pocket and handed them to her. "Here— these are yours, too. Do you want to take it for a ride? Sienna's already in her seat and ready to go."

"I…I don't understand." She glanced from him to the vehicle in utter confusion. Had he just bought her a vehicle that was worth several times her usual salary? And gotten rid of her own car without even asking? "No, I can't accept it. I want my car back."

"Kayla, you and I both know that heap of rust and bolts wasn't going to last for much longer. I didn't like you driving it, especially not with Sienna on board. I've donated it to a trade school where the kids are going to use it as a project car for restoration."

Anger boiled so hot and so fast she thought steam might be coming out of her ears.

"You had no right. I owned that car fair and square. It was mine, not yours to do what you wanted with."

All the joy leeched from Van's face, and inside the car, Sienna began to whimper.

"I wanted you to be safer. All of you," he said firmly. "I did what any responsible adult would have done, and if you were more responsible yourself, you'd see that. Can't you just say thank you, take the keys and move on?"

She understood what he was saying, but that didn't make her any happier. She took a deep breath and forced herself to respond calmly.

"Van, a responsible adult would have sat me down for a conversation about how my car was unsafe for children. Then we could have discussed options for getting it repaired or replaced with something safe but affordable that I'd be comfortable in. Giving away my property without my permission and replacing it with something we both know I would have never chosen for myself isn't responsible—it's dictatorial. I'm not your employee, or one of your troops. You don't have the right to make all the decisions with the expectation that I'll just fall in line."

He looked stricken, which made her soften just a bit. Yes, he'd overstepped—but just how long had it been since there was someone in his life who *wasn't* a subordinate, just waiting to fulfill his orders? He ran a major business and had a lot of people counting on him to make the right decisions. He was used to taking the lead, and that was usually a good thing. Just not now—not here. Not with her.

"I understand that this is an adjustment for you," she continued. "You got thrown in the deep end with parenthood, and you're still trying to figure out how to make this work. And," she admitted, knowing it was only fair for her to admit her flaws, too, "I know that my past hasn't given you a lot of confidence in my ability to make smart decisions for myself. Plus, I've been fighting back on most of your actions since I got here. But I need to know that you're not going to make any more decisions like this—decisions that affect my life and my property—without consulting me. We're in this together, Van. Equal partners. And that means you can't go behind my back like this again. Is that understood?"

"Yes, I…I understand," he said. Then to her shock, he added, "And you're right. I'm sorry. I should have talked to you first. It can't be undone now but it won't happen again."

There was a pause as Kayla, baffled, tried to recall if she'd ever seen Van back down before. Finally she managed to push out a "Thank you."

"Are you up for giving the Audi a try?" he asked.

"I'll try not to hate it," she said teasingly, accepting the keys.

His lips quirked in his signature half smile, making her stomach do a little loop. "Thank you," he said gently.

Kayla got into the driver's seat while Van went around to the passenger side. He showed her how to adjust her seat and mirrors and set them as the driver default setting and instructed her on the features of the car. They were many and varied and Kayla began to wonder if she'd ever remember half the things he told her.

"Guys," she muttered under her breath.

"What's that?"

"Guys," she repeated. "Always about the features. Just tell me how to start the thing, okay?"

Van laughed, and after a quick demonstration of what to do, she put the SUV in gear and backed out of the garage.

The car moved smoothly up the driveway and out the gates. Kayla followed Van's instructions for a short ride around the neighborhood, then back to the house again. Kayla drove into the garage and turned off the engine.

"So, what do you think?" Van asked.

"What do you think I think?" she said, exasperated. "Of course I love it. I'd be mad not to. It drives like a dream, visibility is fantastic and it feels so darn good beneath my hands."

She caressed the leather-covered steering wheel and then the seat on either side of her thighs.

"You don't have to say that—we can trade it in for something else if you'd prefer."

Kayla sighed. "No, it was a good choice. I'll keep it. Thank you, Van. I'll probably spend the next twenty years terrified someone will scratch or steal it, but thank you."

"It has a remote-link antitheft device, so at least you won't have to worry about that."

She rolled her eyes. "Enough with the features. It's very nice and I'm very grateful."

Van nodded in satisfaction. "Good. Then we'll use this to go to the aquarium later?"

"Of course," she said. "There's no reason why not."

"So we're okay now?"

She looked at him, saw the seriousness behind his question reflected in his gaze. "Yes, we're okay."

His shoulders relaxed and his smile was a full one this time. "Good. Then let's go and get ready for the aquarium. I asked Imelda to pack us a picnic so we don't need to rush back."

"You've thought of everything," she said with a sprinkle of acerbity.

"It's what I do," he said simply. "I don't think I'll ever really change—but I can and will work on hearing you out when the situation involves you or the kids. I'll probably fight back pretty hard if we disagree on a situation involving your safety, though."

He was so focused on protecting the people around him. His words made her wonder when anyone, aside from her sister, had ever looked out for him, and she said so.

Van paused in the middle of unclipping Sienna's child restraint. "Why, I do, of course."

"Of course," Kayla repeated and reached out for her daughter. "Come on, Little Miss Muffet. Let's go get you all ready for the fishies, shall we?"

Sienna crowed with glee at the excitement in Kayla's voice, then shouted, "Dadadadad!" at the top of her voice.

"Yes, and your daddy is coming, too."

Van felt a keen sense of belonging that he hadn't experienced before. He wasn't sure how to take it. Or where it fit in his carefully constructed new world. He knew, of course, that once he'd decided to pursue this parenting thing, he would do whatever he could to ensure his children were properly cared for, but he hadn't looked terribly far past that. Suddenly here he was—part of what would appear to be a family outing.

His instincts told him to run for the hills—or at least the office—before it was too late, but a part of him really wanted to actively take part. To soak up Sienna's pleasure in the day. To actually be a dad. No one had ever mentioned how terrifying the prospect truly was. What if something happened? Not that anything had gone wrong so far. Kayla had said the baby was grumpy with her tooth coming through, but he'd seen little enough evidence of it today. In fact, while he'd had that quiet reading time with the child, he'd actually found himself relaxing and enjoying it.

Sienna had been captivated by the selection of pop-up books that were in the basket next to the chair. She selected one after the other herself, then demanded to be lifted into his lap, where she leaned with her warm little back against his stomach and listened as he read the words, then copied him in opening the book flaps. He wasn't sure if she was exceptionally bright for her age or if this was a normal developmental stage for a child, but he experienced an enormous sense of pride in her actions.

Pride, yes, and something else. There was an incredible closeness in having her sit with him—trusting him. He felt as if he would move mountains for her in that moment. Seeing her little fingers reach for the page flaps, listening to her baby babble as she mimicked him reading out loud. Every moment had been incredibly special and it made him realize just how much he'd missed out on already.

Suddenly the idea of shared custody with Kayla held a lot less appeal than it had before. He didn't want to be a part-time father. But maybe he needed to prove that to himself first. This past week he'd been so busy at work he'd stayed back each night as late as he could to get things done. A thought occurred to him. Had it been absolutely necessary that he be the one dotting the *i*'s and crossing the *t*'s? Wasn't that why he'd employed the best of the best in every department of his business, so he could leave when he wanted to?

But he hadn't really wanted to leave work, had he? He'd been staying at the office to avoid seeing Kayla. There, he'd admitted it to himself. What he wasn't prepared to admit just yet was why.

He heard Kayla and Sienna coming back downstairs and went into the foyer to meet them.

"Wow, you don't travel light, do you?" he teased as he relieved Kayla of a large bag she'd slung over one shoulder.

"Not me, her," she replied.

She'd changed into jeans and a colorful long-sleeved cotton top that had tiny mirrors embroidered onto the bodice. It was so her and yet chic at the same time. She was nothing like Dani and he certainly couldn't imagine his sleek business partner toting a baby and a bag with the same air of joy that Kayla seemed to carry inside her. The thought crept into his mind and took him by surprise. Even though he and Dani had planned to take their relationship toward something permanent, they hadn't wanted children, so of course he wouldn't ever have seen her like this. But it was still odd to compare the two women and find his business partner wanting. Dani had been everything he thought he wanted in a life partner. At least, that was what he'd been telling himself for the past year or more.

But she could never be the kind of woman who could simultaneously wipe drool from her child's chin and juggle a hefty tote while walking down stairs. Speaking of heavy totes... Van reached for the bag.

"Jeez, what have you got in here?"

"Just the usual. It's not like you can just sling your

wallet in your back pocket and head out the door with a baby on your hip, you know."

"So I'm learning," he admitted ruefully.

"We need to stop in the kitchen for her bottle, too."

"Already on it. Imelda is putting it in its special container already for us and Jacob has probably already loaded it in the car."

"And her stroller?"

"That's in the car, too. Jacob transferred all your personal effects to the Audi last night. I don't know how you fit all that in your old car. You'll find you have a lot more room in the new one."

Kayla gave him a baleful look. "Van, you've already convinced me to accept the new car, okay? You don't have to keep selling it to me."

He laughed, feeling genuinely lighthearted at their banter. "Good to know you haven't changed your mind in the last twenty minutes."

"I may be female but I'm not that fickle," she said with an exaggerated sniff. "Shall we get this show on the road? The aquarium will be opening soon and I'd rather go through before the crowds build."

In the end, they spent little time at the aquarium. Sienna enjoyed seeing the habitats but the sight of a giant Pacific octopus was enough to start her screaming. Fielding a mixture of concerned and sympathetic looks from the handful of other aquarium patrons, they hurried Sienna back outside. Van tried to soothe her, but ultimately, only Kayla could bring her sobbing to an end. He'd never felt so incredibly helpless in his life. If this was parenthood, he didn't want it.

The instant he thought it, he felt as if he'd betrayed something that ran deep to his moral core. It forced him to rethink, to reassess—and to realize that it wasn't that he didn't want parenthood; it was that he wanted to be the one who could soothe his daughter.

"It was easier when I still nursed her. Sometimes suckling helps her to settle. Can you get her bottle from the bag for me?"

Van reached into the tote and found the insulated container with Sienna's bottle. "Here it is," he said after removing the protective cap.

Kayla looked up gratefully. "Would you like to feed her?"

"Sure," he answered before he could overthink his reply.

"We can go get a seat over there in the shade."

Kayla started walking and Van pushed the stroller in her wake. Once she found a bench seat, she gestured for him to sit down and put Sienna in his lap. For a moment it looked as though Sienna would start up howling again but then Van offered her the bottle and, distracted, the baby grabbed it and began to suck furiously.

"There, that's better, isn't it?" he found himself saying to Sienna.

The baby looked straight up into his eyes and inside him he felt an elemental shift. How could he have considered, even for a moment, not being a part of this—of handing over all care for this wonder of nature, this mini female version of himself, to others to look after?

"She's quite something, isn't she?" Kayla said softly.

She sat down beside him and reached out to brush her fingers over Sienna's hair. "Every day I look at her and I marvel at how she was made and who she's growing up to be."

"She's a little miracle, all right," Van replied, his voice thickening with emotion.

He swallowed it back. He didn't do that kind of thing. He never showed weakness. He remained on the outer fringes, where it was safe, but as Sienna's eyes began to slide shut and she became heavier in his arms, he realized that he had fallen head over heels in love with this precious child. And he hated how vulnerable that made him.

"Should we put her back in the stroller now that she's asleep?" he asked.

"Sure, if you don't want to hold her any longer."

"It's not that—I just thought she might be more comfortable in there."

Kayla looked at him as though she could see right through him to the epiphany that had just occurred and to the terror that closed a cold fist around his heart. He held her gaze, not saying a word. She gave a little sigh and turned to the stroller, adjusting something at the back that lowered the seat into a reclining position.

"There you go. Just pop her in there. We can keep walking around, can't we? You're not in a rush to get back?"

"Sure. I took the day so we could spend it with Sienna. It would be a shame to cut it short."

Through the next hour, they walked from one exhibit to the next. Sienna woke just as they approached the otters, and he was relieved to see she'd slept off her tantrum from before. Then he noticed twin rosy spots had appeared in her cheeks as she slept and he felt a pang of concern.

"Is she all right?" he said, pointing them out to Kayla.

"They're just another symptom of the teething," she said.

Another thing he had no idea about, he reminded himself. The sense of being out of his depth just grew bigger and bigger. How did anyone cope with it? None of the books or articles he'd read had prepared him for the enormity of all of this. It made him wonder why Kayla, who'd always been the quintessential free spirit, had taken on something so big—so *committed*.

"Why did you decide to have Sienna's babies rather than donate the embryos?" he asked.

He realized that it was a question he should have asked her right from the start months ago.

"I thought about it for a long time. It was a scary prospect. You saw how we were living when Sienna died."

He thought back to the crummy apartment Kayla had taken him back to that night after the funeral and nodded.

Kayla continued. "All I could think of was that her children deserved to be born to people who could tell them about just how wonderful their mother was, and my sister deserved to have her one life dream come true, even if it was after she'd gone. I guess it's as simple as that, really."

But it wasn't simple. Kayla's decision had opened

up a whole new can of worms. Worms that invaded his every waking thought and a good many of his sleeping ones, as well.

"But the responsibilities attached," he started. "Didn't you stop to consider them? Don't they scare you?"

"The financial side of things, you mean?" She cocked her head to one side. "I didn't enter it at all lightly. I trained, I worked several jobs, I went without any form of luxury and I saved every penny before the transfer that gave me Sienna. I'd made a long-term plan that would let me have the babies—three, ideally—two years apart. It was only because the storage facility was closing and planning to destroy any embryos that weren't claimed that I was forced to take other action."

"Like approaching me?"

"Like approaching you," she agreed. "I didn't know what to expect when I came to see you, to be honest. I'd hoped that you'd be more open to things."

He mulled over what she'd said. "Would you have told me about the children at all if you hadn't needed my financial aid?"

A look of regret crept into her expression. "No. Probably not."

"Well," he said on a huff of air. "Thank you for being honest about that, at least."

Silence fell between them for a while and then he heard Kayla clear her throat.

"Do you wish I hadn't had Sienna? Or this baby?" she asked, smoothing her top down over her small baby bump. "Do you wish I'd just done nothing and let the embryos be destroyed when the clinic closed down?"

His heart hammered in his chest. A couple of months ago, he'd have said yes and thought nothing of it. But he couldn't even tolerate the thought now that he'd held Sienna, read to her, cleaned her up, fed her…loved her. Loved her? Another shock wave of emotion flooded him. He didn't love. He didn't want to love. He didn't want to ever be that vulnerable to anyone—to be that hurt by anyone—ever again. But he couldn't admit any of that to Kayla, who stood there next to him holding *his* child—one who lived and breathed and grew and learned every second of the day—and be able to keep the emotional distance he knew he needed.

"It's all irrelevant now, isn't it," he heard himself say. "Sienna's here and in a few more months another baby. I'm just glad there weren't more."

He turned away from them both, ignoring Kayla's sharply indrawn breath, and focused on the otters playing in the water in front of them. He was glad there weren't more babies, he kept telling himself, because it was already next to impossible to realize that he loved Sienna. And what if it happened with the next baby, too? Loving this hard, this deeply, made him feel weak, defenseless. He knew better than most how dangerous it was to expose yourself in any way to anyone—be it an unloving adoptive parent or an unseen enemy in an unfriendly land. Could a man's heart honestly grow and expand that big and survive? Could his?

Eleven

For the rest of the outing, Van's vehement words kept playing over and over in her mind. It was her own fault for opening up the conversation in the first place but she certainly hadn't expected such a painfully blunt response. He'd begun to enjoy Sienna, she was sure of it, and his fatherly instincts to provide and protect, though they'd been slow to show, were more than evident now. And yet he'd made it absolutely clear that he didn't want more children. Why? Because of her as their mother?

Her enjoyment of the day was shattered and she found it hard to watch Van and Sienna together without wondering how much he must resent her for having brought the child into his life. When the now-infrequent nausea swept her with unusual ferocity just after they stopped for lunch, she was only too pleased to head home again. At least there she could lock herself away with her hurt and her worries. And maybe dissect where she'd gone so totally and utterly wrong with him.

Should she have told him about the children at all? Well, like he'd said, it was irrelevant now. She couldn't turn back time; she couldn't undo what she'd done even if she wanted to.

Later that night she couldn't sleep at all. No wonder, of course, when she'd ended up napping most of the afternoon away once they'd gotten back to the house. She stepped out onto the balcony outside her room and stared out into the distance. How had her life become so complicated? She'd always kept things so simple—no home, no ties, no responsibilities—all the way up until she realized that her sister's dream of being a mother was going to die along with her.

She'd told herself that she'd done this for her sister, but had she really? Maybe it was all too convenient for her to have her sister's babies. She could build a family without having to build a loving, mature relationship first.

Of course, she'd had relationships, but she'd always prided herself on not settling down in one place with one person for too long. Settling down created expectations that she'd never been prepared to fulfill. Looking back on her life, she could now see how superficial it had been. Oh, sure, she'd worn clothing made from renewable sources; she'd paid extra money to replant a forest wherever she'd traveled to offset her carbon footprint. She'd prided herself on her spontaneity, her ability to live in the moment without structure or planning. But what had that all been for if not to hide from the reality of being a grown-up?

Having Sienna had opened her eyes to a lot of things. Not least of which the idea that making her decisions based on her emotions was not always necessarily the right choice. It certainly hadn't been with Van, had it? How could she have thought it was a good idea to approach him for financial help when she hadn't even done him the most basic courtesy of informing him he was a father?

"It was dumb, dumb, *dumb*," she muttered out loud.

And she was paying the cost now. Not only her, though, but Sienna and Van, too—and possibly even the baby-to-be. The reality of what she'd done to Van and to his life and his plans for his future settled on her shoulders like a ton of lead. There had to be a silver lining in this somewhere, she told herself. Wasn't she the queen of being upbeat and seeing the bright side of everything?

She knew her impulsive nature could sometimes unintentionally cause hurt to people and that her inclination to meddle had led to some tricky situations— case in point, the situation that had blown up with Zoe—but her heart was always in the right place. At least, that was what she'd always told herself. But maybe she'd been wrong all this time. Kidding herself that she was doing things for other people when she was, in reality, doing them for herself and to heck with the consequences.

Her hands gripped the iron railing in front of her and hot tears began to slide down her cheeks. Had she destroyed everything for Van? Ruined any chance he had at future happiness with his children because of her actions? She could have sworn he was falling in love with Sienna, and believing that had made her heart begin to soar for her little girl's future and for that of the baby she carried. But his response to her questions today had made her doubt. Maybe it was too late for him to feel the bond he should have with his children. And if so, it was all her fault.

Had this all been a terrible mistake? No, she couldn't think that. Couldn't assign that awful word to two children she loved more than life itself. And they deserved more. They deserved two loving parents. Preferably ones who were on the same page about their children's futures.

Maybe it would have been simpler if she'd let Van take full custody of the children. But as soon as the thought entered her mind, she felt an overwhelming rejection of it surge through her. No. These were her children, too. She'd cleaned up her act, created stability in her life where before there'd been none, and she had become someone worthy of raising kids—and all for them. She had to believe she'd done the right thing.

Van would come around to that, surely. Wouldn't he?

She stumbled back into her room and closed the French doors to the damp night air before climbing back into her bed. Things had to improve again. They'd already done it once, gone from two people at an impasse to two people who could make compromises. It hadn't been easy and she'd given up a lot of her independence—heck, who was she kidding, pretty much all of her independence, to be honest. Gone was her work, her home, even her car. But she'd gotten plenty in exchange—and best of all were the opportunities for the children. Van could give them things they never could have experienced on just her resources. And he'd made sacrifices, too. Hadn't he broken off his engagement because he had learned he was a father?

Kayla had never stopped to think about what the other woman thought of the sudden change to her future. Right now she felt deeply ashamed. Dani what's-her-name must hate her. She'd had plans for her future with Van. Plans that had been smashed because Kayla didn't stop to think.

She'd created this situation. She had to find a way to make it work. If she didn't, then life would be very dark indeed, and she owed it to her children to make sure the darkness never touched their lives. And she owed it to Van, too.

Kayla noticed that Van made a concerted effort to spend time with Sienna every day, either in the morning or just before her bedtime at seven. But if he was home in the evening, he disappeared into his home office after putting Sienna down and remained there until long after Kayla was tucked up in her bed. At least the time he spent each day with Sienna was an improvement on how things had been before the aquarium day, she consoled herself, even if things between him and Kayla had become more stilted than ever.

So she was surprised to find Van waiting for her when she went downstairs to the kitchen for breakfast one morning two weeks later. He was seated at the kitchen table reading some bound report that he held in one hand while holding a coffee cup in the other. Not for the first time, Kayla found herself briefly mesmerized by his hands. He had beautiful hands for a man. Broad but with long, tapered fingers and with an interesting array of scars she knew he hadn't incurred before he entered the army. They were a reminder that there was so much about him that she didn't know. One day she'd get up the courage to ask him about them, she told herself and forced her gaze away before she could remember other, forbidden, things about those hands and what they were capable of.

"Good morning," she said as brightly as she could. "Late into work?"

"I'm taking you to your doctor's visit today," he said without looking up from his report.

Kayla stopped in her tracks. "Oh, you have time for that?"

The second the words were out of her mouth, she wished them back. Would she ever learn to think first and speak second? She wouldn't blame Van for a minute if he took what she'd said the wrong way.

"I'm sorry," she hastened to add before he could do more than glare at her over the rim of his mug. "I didn't mean it to come out that way. You've been really busy lately, obviously. I didn't expect you'd be able to make it."

"Is that why you didn't tell me about the appointment?"

Kayla felt her cheeks color in shame. To be honest, she hadn't told him about the appointment because she was terrified he'd show no interest in it, or her, and she hadn't wanted to face his rejection. Yes, it was the coward's way out, she fully admitted it, but she absolutely didn't see the point in inviting any more conflict into her life than she'd already created. Seemed she was destined to fail in that department.

He made a gesture with his hand. "Forget I said that. Imelda told me you were scheduled for a scan today. Your notes and everything transferred to an obstetrician in Monterey okay?"

"Yes, I certainly couldn't face the idea of a two-hour drive each way to see the doctor who cared for me through Sienna's gestation. Belle recommended someone."

"Good," he replied, getting up from the table. "It makes sense. Do you know how long the appointment will take?"

She shrugged. "I'm really not sure. I'm due for some tests, and since this is my first time with this doctor, I don't know how long they'll take."

"Tests?" He frowned. "What kind of tests? I thought today was just a routine scan."

"Well, it is. They'll be checking the baby's size and development, especially considering the hyperemesis gravidarum, but they're also doing blood tests and what they call a nuchal translucency test—it's made up of a blood test and the scan where they look to make certain there are no chromosomal abnormalities or other kinds of defects."

Van paled. "And if there are?"

"We'll cross that bridge when we get there," she said with a blitheness she was far from feeling.

"You'd go through with the pregnancy?" he pressed.

She shrugged, but she knew that if faced with that question, she would do what she thought her sister would have done. Bear and love the child no matter what his or her life might look like or how short-lived it might be.

"Like I said—" she tried to smile reassuringly "—we'll deal with it when we know for certain. No point in borrowing trouble."

"You forget, trouble is my business." He got up from the table and put his mug in the dishwasher. "Let me know when you're ready to leave. I'll be in my office."

And like that, he was gone again. Kayla didn't quite know how to feel. A part of her was glad she didn't have to drive herself to the appointment. At least that way, if there was any obvious bad news, she wouldn't be alone. But being with Van lately was akin to cuddling a porcupine, with the exception being that he certainly didn't get that physically close.

* * *

Van watched intently as the image came up on the screen and the sonographer made an indistinct sound.

"Is everything okay?" Van asked, leaning forward.

It was hard to make anything out, but the woman turned to him and smiled. "Just give me a moment or two, Mr. Murphy. I need to complete some measurements and send the information through to Ms. Porter's obstetrician. They'll be able to tell you the outcome."

He shifted in his seat, starting in surprise as Kayla's hand slipped into his.

"It'll be okay, Van. Just relax. There's no reason for anything to be wrong."

But bad things happened all the time. He knew that better than anyone. His fingers tightened around hers and she gave him a reassuring smile before turning her attention to the screen. He was surprised to hear her sniff and looked at her in time to see her surreptitiously wiping away a tear with her other hand.

"What's wrong?" he asked, feeling more terrified than he had been a moment ago.

"Nothing," she said through more tears. "It's just such a crazy miracle, isn't it? Look, you can see it there on the screen."

"And here's the heartbeat," the sonographer said.

The room was filled with a rapid drumming sound.

"Is that okay? It seems very fast," Van asked, staring hard at the screen.

"All perfectly normal," came the steady reply. She adjusted a setting on the equipment and the resolution of the image on the screen sharpened. "I see you've requested to know the baby's sex, if possible, so let's have a look here. And there he is."

"It's a boy?" Kayla asked, squeezing Van's hand so tight it actually hurt.

"He's being very accommodating and showing off, so, yes, it's definitely a boy. Congratulations. Was that what you were hoping for?"

"I didn't care. I just wanted another healthy baby. Don't you feel the same, Van?"

But he was beyond answering. First a daughter and now a son? This for a man who'd decided never to have children, who never expected to be a father? Emotion threatened to drown him and he focused on the pain of Kayla's fingernails digging into the palm of his hand. Allowed the discomfort to distract him from the crazy swirl of joy and fear and exhilaration that made his eyes burn and his chest ache.

Through the buzzing in his ears, he heard Kayla speaking to the sonographer.

"He's a bit overwhelmed. He missed out on the scans with our daughter, so this is all new to him."

"I understand," the woman said with a smile in his direction.

She turned her attention back to her equipment and continued with the various measurements she had to make. Van was fascinated—the tiny skull with the tiny brain developing inside it, the curve of the spinal cord, the limbs. This was a little human. A child. *His* son.

"Is he sucking his thumb?" Van asked.

"He certainly is."

"Wow."

Kayla had called it a crazy miracle and she wasn't wrong. It was almost beyond his comprehension seeing the image on the screen and correlating it to the fact the baby was nestled in her womb. And he'd wanted to miss out on all of this? But there was still the issue of his parents' DNA to contend with. What if his son, or Sienna, carried that same disposition to self-destruct by using substances? He had such a responsibility to see to it that they weren't tempted to go down that road and potentially destroy their lives. Lives that Kayla had fought so hard to ensure they had without realizing what kind of time bomb they could be carrying. These babies, his children, deserved his best. Could he give it to them? Would he be enough?

Those questions played on his mind for the balance of the day. He locked himself in his office in an attempt to avoid them, but it was useless. After a long video call with Dani regarding an ongoing and escalating issue with one of their clients in the Middle East, Van shut down his computer and pushed away from his desk. It was dark outside and far later than he'd realized. That was why he and Dani had always been so well suited, he thought. Both prepared to keep going to get the job done, no matter the hour. Would he still be able to continue to give his work everything with two children in the house? It was unlikely.

Life, as he'd made it, had begun to change irrevocably and he hated to admit it, but he was scared. He could count on one hand the number of times he'd felt this way before. The first time his adoptive father had lifted a hand to him, the first time he'd been deployed and the first time he'd seen active duty. But this was a whole new kettle of fish.

Van stretched and heard the kinks in his back crack. A swim would be a good idea about now, he decided. Maybe a few lazy laps of the pool would help ease some of the jittering sensation that danced along his nerves so insistently. Yeah, some mindless exercise was just what he needed.

It was a beautiful night. The air was cool but the pool felt like warm silk on her skin as she went down the steps and was submerged in its softness. Kayla flipped onto her back and floated for a while, staring up into the cloudless night sky. Even with the subtle pool lighting she could still see more stars than she could count. It made her feel as if she was in another world altogether. In so many ways, that was true.

She sensed rather than heard a movement by the side of the pool and turned her head to look. Van stood at the edge. Moonlight limning his powerful physique made him look almost ethereal. Something deep inside her clenched before releasing slowly on a wave of hunger that had nothing to do with food and everything to do with the man standing there, silent as a statue.

"Did you want the pool to yourself?" she asked, treading water now at the deeper end of the pool. "I can go in now."

"No, don't leave on my account."

His voice was gruff and he stayed there—standing

still. She couldn't tear her eyes off him. She tracked the shadowed lines of muscle along his shoulders and her mouth went dry, forcing her to swallow convulsively. She tried to avert her gaze, but it was useless. She might be pregnant but she was first and foremost a woman and most certainly a woman with an eye of appreciation for a stark male beauty such as his.

Any male's? a voice inside her asked. *Or just his?*

She couldn't lie to herself. Her attraction specifically to him went deep. Physically, Van was perfection. And emotionally? She wasn't sure yet. So much had changed between them and yet still remained the same. When they were growing up, he'd always been the one looking out for her. Making decisions regarding her safety and bailing her out of difficulties when she slipped through his protective net. They'd always had a relationship, of sorts, she admitted. But it had been lopsided—at least to her way of thinking. He'd never respected her or viewed her as an equal. She'd thought she had a chance to balance it after Sienna died and look how that had worked out, she reminded herself. But now, well, this was another place in time. Maybe this time things could be different.

She felt a flush of heat build from her chest and work its way up to her cheeks. Kayla was glad for the darkness. She still hadn't gotten around to buying a new swimsuit, and believing she'd be alone tonight, she hadn't covered herself in a T-shirt before entering the water. Right now, unable to resist the magnetic attraction she felt toward Van, she felt as if her body was bursting from her bikini—and the slide of the water against her made her feel naked. Naked and Van were probably not a good combination in her head at the moment, but as hard as she tried to stop them, nerve endings all through her body sprang to life in the most persistent fashion. The pool, which had only seconds ago been a sanctuary of peace and tranquility, now transformed into a simmering melting pot of need.

She continued to watch him as he dove neatly into the pool and began to swim freestyle. One lap, then another, until she lost count. She felt a prick of chagrin that he could so easily ignore her and was on her way to the stairs at the shallow end when he surfaced beside her.

"Not swimming anymore?" he asked.

"I've pretty much been just floating. It's relaxing, but I should probably leave you to it," she said, doing her best not to stare at him.

His hair was plastered to his head and water ran in rivulets down his face, his neck and then his chest. Desire pulled with such a hard wrench from her core that she gasped with its intensity. If she could only reach out, touch him. Let her fingers trace the lines of his body. No! They'd already gone down that road once and look where that had ended, she told herself. Distraction. She needed distraction and latched on to the one thing she knew would drive any thought of sex from her mind.

"I think you're going to be a great dad, Van," she blurted. "I just wanted to say that."

He looked startled, as if that was the last thing he'd

expected her to say. He inclined his head in acknowledgment but didn't say a word. Instead he kept looking into her eyes, perhaps trying to delve beyond her
clumsy attempt at deflection and get straight to the
burning-hot center of her. It made her feel an urge to
fill the silence.

"Did you enjoy today?" she asked. "Seeing the
new baby?"

A tiny frown pulled at his brows. "*Enjoy* is probably not the right word for it," he said. "But it was
fascinating." His eyes dropped from her face to her
belly—to where his son was nestled. "And terrifying
at the same time."

"I know what you mean. The first time I saw
Sienna, I freaked. I mean, I never planned to have
kids, and when I decided to have her, I didn't stop
to think about every aspect of it. I just knew I had
to fulfill my promise and planned to do that without
considering all the aspects of it."

Van snorted a laugh. "That's so like you."

She allowed herself a smile. "I've done a lot of stupid things in my life. I just wanted to do something
right for a change. Something where I put someone
else's needs and hopes first. But I still kind of leaped
in with both feet. I guess I haven't changed much,
have I? But then, neither have you."

"You don't think I've changed? I thought I had. A
lot." He sounded mildly disappointed.

She looked at him. Of course he was different now
than he'd been as a boy. He'd achieved wealth and
authority beyond what anyone could have expected.

But essentially he hadn't changed at all. He was still the protector, still distant from everyone around him even while making sure they were all okay. She'd seen that reserved demeanor of his completely crack just the once. The night they'd made love after her sister's funeral. He'd been more open with her then than he'd ever been. With their bodies, they'd said all the things that their minds couldn't formulate words for, and in a mutual need for comfort, they'd clung to one another and soared to exquisite heights of pleasure in their bid to obliterate their grief.

"Changed?" she repeated, musing on the word. "You're maybe more driven than you were. You've obviously come a long way since leaving the army, that's for sure. It's not every man who creates an empire in the time you have."

"I'm lucky that my skill set translates to a very high-value commodity. People need security, and in the countries where we work, those people are prepared to pay an extremely high price for it. Besides, I didn't do it all on my own. I was fortunate to be able to recruit a pool of people with skills that complement mine."

"People like Dani? What skills did she bring to the table?" Kayla asked, then hated herself for perversely bringing the other woman into their conversation.

"Her company provides the electronics that make our job a whole lot easier. If I'd had to invest separately in development for that side of things, I certainly wouldn't be where I am now."

"I'm sorry you two didn't work out."

Kayla knew the words were a lie the moment she spoke them. She wasn't sorry at all. There'd been something so unfeeling about the other woman when they'd met, something so clinical and detached. Sure, she was stunning, but in the same way a cool marble sculpture could be stunning and yet cold, empty.

"We still work well together despite that," Van replied.

Somehow that seemed to be a shame. There should have been some fire between them, surely. If Kayla had been so close to a person that she'd considered marrying him just to have it fall apart, she knew she wouldn't have been able to calmly keep working with him. It seemed especially wrong that it had happened with Van. She knew how deep his passion lay. The kind of man he was with Dani Matthews felt false. As if he was fitting himself into a mold where he thought he ought to be, instead of going where he truly belonged. But hadn't he always been like that? As a boy, as a soldier? He'd delivered on expectations every time but when had he had an opportunity to truly be himself?

The thought brought her back to their one night, to the raw honesty they'd expressed in actions when words were no longer enough. Usually she tamped down her thoughts of that time, but right now they flared, hot and bright, to the forefront of her mind. Her body, already simmering, fired to life.

"I know I couldn't," she commented.

"Why not?"

"I guess because I feel too much. I'm not the kind of person who can compartmentalize my emotions and my needs so easily. If the man I wanted to marry broke off our engagement for the same reasons you did..." Her voice trailed away and she shook her head. No, she didn't want to go down that road.

"You'd what?" he prompted.

"Well, if he really meant anything to me and I thought we stood a chance together, I'd fight tooth and nail for him. I'd learn to compromise, to blend his wishes with my own—especially if his children were involved."

"And you think Dani didn't fight for me?"

Ah, now, there was a thought. Maybe she'd been too dismissive of the beautiful Ms. Matthews.

"Did she?" Kayla countered, suddenly curious.

"Not beyond our initial discussion, no."

"But you guys were in love, right?"

He dunked his head under the surface and rose back up again, pushing the water from his eyes with his hands. "Love didn't enter into it. It didn't have to."

"Then I'm sorry for you, and for her."

"Don't be. We're adults. It hasn't hurt our working arrangements."

"But don't you see? That's what's wrong. It should hurt—your heart, your mind. Everything!" Kayla argued.

"And that's your philosophy on life?"

"It's my philosophy on love."

"Then it's just as well you're not in love, isn't it. It sounds very painful to me."

His words couldn't have struck her any harder than if he'd slapped her.

"Are you saying you don't feel?"

"Not if I don't choose to."

"You still keep a wall between you and the rest of the world, don't you? I've only seen you take that wall down once."

"What are you talking about?"

"Our night together," she said passionately. "I know you felt that night. Be honest. You were hurting. I know I was. And, just for a while, we both made the hurt go away. We *felt* something together. Something that was bigger than the hurt, something that was special. Don't you ever think about it? Don't you want to feel like that again?"

"No, I absolutely do not. That night was nothing but a mistake."

He launched toward the edge of the pool and hauled himself out, distancing himself from the conversation both mentally and physically. The way he always did from anything that approached emotion, she reminded herself. She shouldn't feel as though she'd lost something precious, but she did. By the time Kayla got out of the pool and wrapped herself in the toweling robe she'd brought down with her, he was gone.

She'd never learn, she thought as she made her way up to her room. Always blurting stuff out. Well, at least it made life interesting, she consoled herself, as opposed to the frozen wasteland that was Van's chosen emotional spectrum. She closed her bedroom door behind her and leaned back against it, feeling loss and sorrow seep through her. A knock on the wooden surface behind her made her start. She turned to open the door.

Van stood there, a towel wrapped at his waist and a smoldering green fire burning in his eyes.

"Van?"

"I do think about that night. I think about how your hair smelled, how your skin felt beneath my hands, the taste of you on my tongue, about the heat of your body when I was inside you, and all of it drives me crazy. I can't stop thinking about that night. Or you."

And then he reached for her.

Twelve

His hands grasped her shoulders and he tugged her toward him. Stunned, she offered no resistance. His lips were hot and dry as they descended on hers. A bolt of desire, searing and desperate, shuddered through her as their lips met, as his tongue swept across the seam of her mouth. She parted her lips on a cry of need and he wasted no time deepening the kiss.

Kayla's hands flew to his head, her fingers driving through his short dark hair, her nails gently scraping his scalp. He groaned into her mouth and the sound felt as though it vibrated throughout her entire body. She could already feel the press of his hips against her. Feel the hardness that spoke of his need for her. Inside, she turned molten.

A maelstrom of sensation poured through her

as he wrenched free the knot in her robe's belt and pushed aside the lapel to expose her to his starving gaze. His hand shook as he reached for the neck tie of her bikini. One quick tug and the too-small triangles of damp fabric fell to her waist. With one finger he traced a faint blue vein on her swollen breast, then followed it with the tip of his tongue.

She tried to speak, to tell him how he made her feel, but the second his mouth closed around her nipple, words failed her. Her knees threatened to buckle and send them both crashing to the floor. As if he sensed her weakness, he scooped her into his arms and carried her next to the bed and put her gently down on her feet again. Three more flicks of his fingers and her bikini top was off and her bottoms had fallen in a heap on the carpet. Her robe followed. Then his towel.

Kayla traced her hands over his chest, down his rib cage and lower to the waistband of his swimming shorts. Her fingers closed over the bulge at the front and he dropped his head to the crook of her neck. One of his hands closed over hers, halting her when she would have squeezed him.

His voice shook. "I want you, Kayla, but if you don't want this, too, say it now while I can still, maybe, leave this room."

"Want you? I need you, Van. Here. *Now*," she whimpered.

He felt like he'd waited a millennium to hear those words and he didn't waste the invitation she offered.

He bent his head to kiss her again and pulled her hard to his body. She felt just as perfect against him as she had the last time. His world had been tilted off its axis for so long. But here, now, things finally felt so very right.

His hands skimmed over her body, different now than before. A voice inside him told him he should be ashamed that he was so turned on by the lushness of her new curves, by the fact that she was carrying his child, but then he realized the voice wasn't his. It was merely an echo of disapproval from far in his past. An echo that deserved to be erased forever because nothing—absolutely nothing—had ever felt as right as holding Kayla in his arms did now.

She was spectacular, her skin smooth and warm. He coaxed her down onto the mattress so he could see all of her, touch all of her, taste all of her. She was no passive partner in this. Her hands reached for him, squeezing, tracing, stroking until his skin was burning and his entire body shook with need. But he'd waited what felt like forever for this. He didn't want to rush it now.

He settled over her, bearing his weight on his arms.

"Are you okay with this?" he rasped as he bent his head to tease the tip of one pale pink nipple with his tongue.

"I'd be a lot more okay if you'd hurry up," she said, squirming against him. "And if you'd remove those wet shorts of yours."

"They're the only thing keeping me under control," he admitted as he smiled against her skin, loving the fact that she was so impatient for him. "And I meant with having me on top of you."

"I'm more than okay. You're just perfect, right where you are."

She thrust her hips against his groin again and groaned deep in the back of her throat. He could see the hot flush of desire on her skin and the glitter in her eyes as she looked at him.

"Don't take forever about this, soldier," she said teasingly.

"I'll take…just…as…long…as…I…take," he answered, punctuating each word with a nip or a lick of her breasts.

Her nipples had hardened and distended and he could have spent forever paying homage to her physical perfection. A lifetime wouldn't be long enough to spend following the tracery of veins that glowed palest blue beneath her skin. To spend holding her breasts, gently squeezing those pink peaks and laving them with his tongue. Kayla's nails dug into his shoulders, spurring him to take as much time as he could to make this good for her.

But there was more of her to explore, to pleasure, and he was nothing if not dedicated. Beneath his hands, her rib cage felt so small and her skin pebbled with goose bumps as he traced his tongue over each rib, then followed the center line between them before finishing at her belly button. The thickening of her waist and the slight rise of her tummy were more noticeable lying down. An incredible sense of strength and pride fought through the haze of desire that wreathed him. His child. His woman.

"Van?" Her voice sounded unsure and he realized he'd been motionless for a minute or more. "Are you okay? Is everything all right?"

"Everything is perfect," he said through a throat that had suddenly clogged with emotion. "You are perfect."

Then he bent his head again, lower this time, to the neat thatch of blond curls at the apex of her thighs, then lower still to where her musky wetness called to him. Kayla's thighs were trembling as they fell wider apart, allowing him to nestle between them, to feel their silky softness against the breadth of his shoulders.

He blew a cool stream of air against her glistening flesh and smiled as he heard the hitch in her labored breathing.

"Van Murphy, if you think you're going to tease me now…" she threatened, closing her fingers in his short-cropped hair.

But he was far too much of a gentleman to keep her waiting. He nuzzled her tender spot and felt her thighs tighten around him.

"Yes, please. Right there."

Her voice shook and he drew pleasure from the fact that he could make her feel so much. This woman, who was the light to his darkness, who was his polar opposite in so many things but who was his perfect match in bed. Van swirled his tongue around her clitoris, increasing the pressure with each moment and then easing it off. Kayla was begging him incoherently to give her the release he knew boiled just beneath the surface and it took every ounce of his considerable self-control to keep her teetering on that edge before he closed his mouth around her and sucked hard, flicking his tongue against the swollen bud.

Beneath him, Kayla's hips rose involuntarily from the bed and her whole body tensed as the first wave hit her. He almost came in his shorts, her orgasm was so intense. Watching her, knowing he'd given her this pleasure, this moment of mindlessness beyond measure, made him feel stronger than anything he'd ever done before in his life. His shorts were an unwelcome constriction and he finally shucked them off. His erection, thick and heavy and aching so hard that he wondered if he'd be able to hold on as long as necessary, sprang free.

Van shifted, moving higher up Kayla's body, positioning himself at her entrance. The sensation of her core's heat against the sensitive head of his penis almost sent him hurtling over the brink. He paused, pulling on every ounce of reserve he had left.

"I don't want to hurt you," he stated.

"For goodness' sake, just make love to me, Van," Kayla demanded, her voice sounding drunk on bliss and need.

Her hands were at his hips, the heels of her feet pressing on his buttocks as he slid inside her. A massive shudder shook his body as he sank full length inside. This was home, he realized. Not a house, not a place. But this woman, this moment, together.

He began to move, his hips thrusting with more vigor on each stroke. Kayla's inner muscles tightened around him, increasing the intensity of his pleasure until with a cry she came undone again, her orgasm seeming to take control of them both as it pulled him over the edge and into a searing pleasure so powerful he felt as though his climax could go on into eternity.

The ripples of satisfaction were still running through him as he collapsed on the bed to her side and rolled her over him, still joined.

"If that's the last thing I ever feel for the rest of my days, I'll die a happy woman," Kayla said against his chest before kissing him there. "I love you, Van."

Her voice was thick, heavy, and within seconds she was asleep. Van lay there listening to her breathing, cradling her in his arms and waiting for his heart rate to return to some semblance of normal. But in the wake of her declaration, he knew that would be impossible. This should have been the moment when he felt at peace, but for some irrational reason, he'd never felt less peaceful in his life. The urge to get up and leave her was strong. He didn't do this kind of thing, this depth of emotion, this level of connection to anyone. She loved him. He couldn't—wouldn't—love her. It was too much and too terrifying to contemplate. It left a person too open, too raw, too exposed.

His brain tried to argue with him. This moment with her, her declaration, it was too much to lose—*she* was too much, meant too much. Maybe he'd always known that deep down, always sensed that Kayla was the one who could make him this vulnerable inside. Make him want things he'd told himself it was safer to live without. She made him begin to believe that he deserved these things—a family, a rich life, love. But he knew he didn't. All it would take was one slip. He'd screw it up eventually—people with his background always did.

She shifted a little in his arms and the warm puffs of her breath against his chest were painfully endearing. It would be all too easy to stay here, to wake with her later and to explore their sensual journey together over and over.

He had the sense that the walls were closing in on him. That he was being buried in a mire of emotion he had no idea how to handle. He knew he couldn't do it. It had been a mistake the first time he'd made love with her and it had been a mistake this time, too. He couldn't give her what she wanted, what she deserved. He would always let her down in the long run. It might as well be sooner rather than later, he decided as he gently extricated himself from her arms and slid from the bed, pausing a moment to pull the covers over her.

He picked up his towel and damp shorts from the floor and headed for the door. It wouldn't have lasted between them anyway, even if he had been willing to try—he knew that. Nothing good ever did. Van flicked off the light switch and closed the door behind him.

Kayla woke the next morning and stretched languorously, reaching one arm over to stroke Van's back. But her hand met nothing but cool sheets. It didn't bother her at first. She knew he was an early riser and she'd become a late one recently with either Belle or Imelda getting Sienna up in the mornings. That would have to stop, she decided. It wasn't fair to Belle to make her handle mornings when she was on call all night. And Kayla was feeling so much better now that she could take over her duties as Sienna's mom properly again. Actually, today in particular she was feeling exceptionally well. She smiled and stretched again before swinging her legs over the side of the bed and getting up.

There was an energy surging in her body right now that made her want to step out onto her balcony, throw her arms out to the world and give thanks for the exceptional lovemaking she'd had with Van. That she was stark naked and that she could spy Jacob working the garden on the perimeter of the property were two very good reasons not to, she thought with a private smile.

She went to her bathroom and quickly showered and dressed for the day—eager to see Van and maybe suggest another family outing. Now that she'd admitted to herself and to him that she loved him, she wanted to explore those feelings further and, if possible, to coax his feelings out of him. The fact he'd come to her last night was a revelation. For once he'd put aside the distant businessman and become purely the man. And what a man. She still tingled and throbbed in the parts of her body that hadn't experienced such rich sensual pleasure in a very long time.

Kayla skipped downstairs and went to the kitchen.

As she approached, she heard Imelda coaxing Sienna to eat her cereal.

"Good morning!" Kayla said.

She went straight to her daughter's high chair and plonked a kiss on the top of Sienna's head.

"Good morning to you, too, Ms. Porter. You're obviously feeling on top of the world today." Imelda smiled back.

"I am. And I'm starving. I might even manage two slices of toast today," she answered with a wink. Kayla then looked around. "Is Van around? I thought he might like to go out with Sienna and me today."

"No, Ms. Porter. He left while it was still dark."

A cold, sick sensation rippled through her. A sensation that was rapidly chased by a series of questions. He left? Where to? When? Why had he gone without saying goodbye?

"He didn't mention anything about that to me. Did you know he was going away?" She was proud of the fact that none of her shock filtered through her voice.

"Not in advance, no. Some emergency overseas, apparently."

"Doesn't he have staff to deal with things like that?"

"You know Mr. Murphy. Always with the personal attention to detail. He takes a lot of pride in his work."

"So where did he go?"

Imelda mentioned a well-known trouble spot and Kayla felt a fist of fear clutch her heart. "So you see," Imelda concluded, "he wouldn't have sent a staff member into an area like that. It's such a volatile region and he's always said he'd never send anyone anywhere he wasn't prepared to go himself."

Wouldn't he? Kayla asked herself. Or had he, in the face of her declaration, just grabbed hold of an opportunity to run away—like he always did? With no goodbye, no message of when he'd be back. Tears burned in the back of her eyes and her throat choked on emotion. She thought he'd changed, that he was prepared to live up to his responsibilities here—to her, to his children. But she'd been so very wrong.

"He'll miss Sienna's first birthday," she said bitterly.

Imelda nodded. "I know."

How could he do this? Leave now after everything they'd shared? Kayla automatically went through the motions of putting her breakfast together but found she had no appetite at all when it came to eating it. She felt as if all the sunshine had suddenly fled her world. It was the past repeating all over again. Why, though? she asked over and over. Even if he wasn't ready to pursue something with her, why would a man deliberately put himself in danger when he didn't have to and when he had a responsibility to children here at home? It didn't make sense to her at all. His children needed him in their lives. Not just as some transient male role model who turned up from time to time, but as a father who would guide them and love them and teach them about life and living it.

None of it made sense at all. He was the one who'd threatened to take both kids from her. He was the one who'd ensconced them here in this house and took over her life. He was the one who'd come to her last night and who'd made love to her like a man who felt love, not fear of where love would lead.

On the heels of her sorrow at discovering he'd gone came a sudden rise of burning anger. How dare he? He'd changed the parameters of their relationship with his actions last night—he had no right to renege on that by morning. And his duty to Sienna—how could he expect to swan in and out of her little world and *choose* to go somewhere from where he might not return?

Kayla had no trouble feeding the flames of her fury. In fact, they buoyed her through her day and the days that followed until Van's return. The sweet, passionate, loving night they'd spent together was nothing but a distant memory two weeks later when he finally returned home, and she wasted no time cornering him in his office.

He was pale with exhaustion and still dressed in dusty fatigues, his T-shirt stretched across the broadness of his shoulders and his chest like a second skin.

"So," she started without even a greeting. "You decided to stop hiding."

Her words and tone were as sharp as shattered glass. It was no more than he deserved.

"Hello to you, too," he replied, looking up from a stack of papers that had been couriered from his office in San Francisco earlier that day.

"Why, Van?"

He continued to look at her, drinking in her beauty.

Even as angry as she clearly was, she pulled at him like a powerful magnet. A magnet he'd tried to ignore when he'd chosen to leave the way he had. The similarities between that night and their first together hadn't escaped him. He'd slipped away like a thief in the night, telling himself it was for the best even while his heart argued that he should stay. But then, he'd long since gotten accustomed to ignoring his heart.

"What?" she prompted, folding her arms across her midsection. The look she gave him should have withered him on the spot. "Got nothing to say? Well, that's just dandy because I have plenty."

He stood there and took it as she unleashed her wrath with guns blazing. He'd earned it, every word, every accusation, and he hated every second of it—especially when she brought up Sienna's birthday, which had been last week. He honestly hadn't known—hadn't bothered to find out. But it hurt to realize he'd missed it. Not that he'd ever show it.

It was one thing to come to a moment of truth by yourself; it was quite another to have it hurled at you. And everything inside him urged him to fight back. To tell her the truth. But he couldn't find the words to say that he wasn't enough for someone like her and he never would be.

"Are you quite finished?" he said when she finally wound down.

There were tear tracks on her face and he battled himself to ignore the deep regret that shafted him, together with the knowledge that he was the one solely responsible for putting them there.

"I'll be finished when you can admit that you choose to deliberately put your life in danger rather than face up to your issues!" she raged once more. "I'm guessing you ran away because I told you I love you. Well, guess what—that's not the worst thing that could happen to you. You won't die because someone loves you—or because *I* love you. You don't have to always be the hard man, the defender of the weak. You are allowed to show weaknesses yourself and to be vulnerable to another person, someone you can trust—like me."

"You don't know what you're talking about. I didn't run away. I had work to do," he said dismissively, even though he knew he was lying.

She hadn't said anything that he hadn't already thought of himself these past two weeks. But he wasn't ready to admit that to anyone—not now, not ever. That would mean opening up a part of himself that had been locked down and secured far too long for him to even consider changing. Not for her, not for anyone.

He continued, deliberately choosing the words that would push her away. "I wasn't running away from issues. I was running away from you."

She whitened and appeared to sway a little under the cruelty of his words. Van fought back every instinct to claw the words back, to apologize, to put out a hand to steady her when she was so obviously shaken. Instead he remained very firmly where he was.

"I see," she said quietly. "Well, thank you for being honest about that, at least."

She turned and walked away. Van's fists clenched tight at his sides, every muscle in his body locked as he held back the need to follow after her. It was better this way, he kept telling himself. She couldn't love him; he wouldn't let her. As vicious as he'd been, it was the right thing to do. It had to be because if it wasn't, then he'd just sent away the best thing that had ever happened to him his whole miserable life.

Thirteen

Loving a man who didn't love you and never would was a great deal more painful than Kayla could ever have imagined. Oh, sure, she'd had crushes on boys growing up, boys who hadn't returned the favor, but this was another thing entirely. It left her heart sore and miserable to the extent that it was an effort to be upbeat for Sienna each day. Even Imelda had noticed, and between her and Belle, they seemed to be hell-bent on trying to cheer her up. But this wasn't just a funk; this felt like the end of everything she'd never known she'd really wanted. And she wanted out.

She'd admitted to herself that despite everything, she truly wanted a real, permanent relationship with Van. But now she knew it to be an impossible dream. And living here, sitting across the table from him on the nights he was home for dinner or watching him spend time with Sienna, coaxing her to walk on her chubby little legs, was killing her inside. He'd never love her—she accepted that now—and she wasn't about to be a moth to his flame until she drove herself senseless with it. But she had to be here to fulfill the terms of their contract, even though staying in his house was a living hell—when he was here anyway, she reminded herself glumly.

Van was gone again on business—safely stateside this time, to her untold relief—when Imelda called her to the phone.

"Who is it?" Kayla asked as she reached for the handset Imelda held toward her.

"Ms. Matthews," the housekeeper answered with a sour twist to her mouth.

There weren't many people that Imelda disapproved of but there was no mistaking the antipathy reflected on her normally jovial face right now.

"Did she say what she wanted?"

"She didn't deign to tell me," Imelda sniffed.

Kayla took the call off hold and said hello.

"Kayla, I trust you're well?" The other woman's faultlessly modulated tones came down the line.

Kayla stifled the urge to rub her ear. "I'm fine, thank you. Van's not here right now. Did you want to leave a message for him with me?"

"No, it's you I wanted to speak to." Dani paused a moment before continuing. "I wondered if you and I could meet and have a chat. Perhaps tomorrow morning at Fisherman's Wharf in Monterey, say eleven thirty?"

Kayla couldn't hold back her surprise. "Why?"

"Let's discuss that then. Can I take it that you're amenable to that time and place? I trust you'll be able to find a babysitter."

Who the heck used words like *amenable* in conversation, Kayla thought before answering. Imelda, who could hear the conversation, rolled her eyes before nodding her assent.

"Yes, that's not a problem. Eleven thirty it is, then."

Dani mentioned the name of a restaurant and then ended the call.

"Mark my words," Imelda said taking the phone back from Kayla. "She's up to no good."

"I have to admit I'm surprised she wants to see me. What on earth do we have in common?"

"Mr. Murphy," Imelda replied with a fiery look in her eye.

"Oh, no, but we're not... He's not... It's not like that between us."

Imelda merely raised her brows.

"It's not," Kayla repeated adamantly. "Well, I guess I'll find out soon enough what she wants. Are you sure you'll be okay with Sienna tomorrow? I know Belle is on a rostered day off but I'm sure she wouldn't mind having her for a couple of hours. She told me she had no plans for tomorrow but lazing around the pool and reading a book."

"Shush now—you know I love to have Sienna to myself. But just you be careful around that woman. I don't trust her. It's not natural for a woman to be so—" She broke off and searched for the right word. "So soulless."

"Soulless?" Kayla asked with a frown. "I only met her the once and she struck me as very…" she tried to think of a nice word for *cold* and settled on "…self-possessed, but she can't be all that bad. She and Van were going to get married, weren't they?"

"Believe me, that woman never does or says anything that isn't in her personal interests. She has a calculator where her heart should be. It was a good thing when Mr. Murphy broke their engagement and confined their relationship to business only."

"You didn't think they suited one another?" Kayla knew she shouldn't be prompting Imelda to gossip, but she couldn't resist.

"On the surface, maybe, but she could never give him what he needs. Not like you can."

Kayla shook her head. "Oh, no. He doesn't want anything from me."

"Like a lot of men, he doesn't know what he needs. He's too busy looking out for everyone else to ever think about looking out for himself. You say he doesn't want anything from you—what's more to the point is that he doesn't want to want anything from anybody. And wanting is one thing, but needing is entirely another. He needs *you*. You should think on that," Imelda said.

Kayla found herself watching Imelda's back as she left the room and turned over the other woman's words in her mind. Imelda couldn't have been serious. Kayla had nothing to offer Van. Nothing he would admit to needing, anyway. As much as she hoped it could be possible for them to forge a new beginning together, he'd made it blatantly clear that it would never happen. Which left her wondering what the heck Dani wanted to talk to her about.

The next day, Dani was already waiting at the table when Kayla arrived at the restaurant. She stood and shook Kayla's hand when she approached. The nerves that had skittered and danced in the pit of her stomach tightened into an uncomfortable knot. She'd been feeling queasy again all morning. There was no doubt that a lot of her discomfort came from nerves right now. She'd considered canceling but believed if she put Dani off, she'd only have to reschedule, because she had a feeling that Dani was persistent once she wanted something.

"Please, sit," Dani directed. "What would you like to drink?"

"Just filtered iced water for me, please."

"Of course." Dani smiled in return and gestured for one of the waiters to take their drinks order.

Once he was gone, Dani turned her full attention on Kayla. Kayla studied her. She hadn't changed at all from the first time Kayla had seen her—still impeccably groomed and with her hair a perfect glossy swing about the china-doll perfection of her face. It made Kayla want to reach for her more tousled locks and try to tame them into some semblance of order but she forced herself to keep her hands still.

"I imagine that you're wondering why I called you."

Kayla could only nod.

"I want Donovan back, and you're going to help me get him," she said in a tone that, while perfectly pleasant, held undertones that made Kayla uncomfortable.

"I don't see how I have any influence in the matter. Van very much does as he pleases," Kayla replied as evenly as she could.

Dani smiled at her condescendingly, much as one would to a particularly dense person. "I thought you'd say as much. Let's be honest here. You and I both know that Donovan is miserable with the current state of affairs."

"I wouldn't say miserable, exactly," Kayla defended, but she knew he wasn't happy. There'd been a cloud hanging over him since their night together that made him more distant than ever.

"There's no point in lying to yourself," Dani continued. She waved her slender ringless hands extravagantly. "He made a commitment based on an emotional reaction to a situation that took him completely by surprise and he's too honorable to step away from it, even though he knows it's a huge mistake. It's up to you and me to make it right."

Dani reached into an impossibly elegant narrow leather briefcase and pulled out a thin sheaf of papers, which she then slid across the table to Kayla.

"I'd like you to look over this. I think you'll find the terms quite agreeable."

Kayla picked up the papers and read through the document. It was pretty clear, despite the legal jargon contained inside. Dani was offering her money, a great deal of money, to move out of Van's home and away to another city. In return, all she had to do was promise not to contact Van again. On paper, it all looked quite simple and straightforward but everything in Kayla revolted at the idea. Even though she knew she had no future with Van, what about the children? What about his relationship with them?

An all-too-familiar sick feeling bloomed in her stomach. She reached for her iced water and took a sip to try to settle her nerves but it was no use.

"Excuse me," she blurted and rose to her feet.

Kayla let the papers fall to the table and rushed toward where she'd seen the restrooms. Once there, her stomach convulsed, forcing her to lose the light breakfast she'd eaten a couple of hours ago and leaving her feeling weak and wrung out. With shaking hands, she flushed the toilet and went to the basin and washed her hands, running cold water over her wrists for some time before grabbing a paper towel, moistening it, and wiping her face and the back of her neck before the nausea could swell again.

Her eyes swam with the words printed on the agreement Dani had presented to her. It was painfully clear-cut. Dani wanted her to leave Van, and she was prepared to pay richly for what she wanted. Kayla would have unfettered access to a trust fund established for her and the children and the security of a fully serviced apartment to help her so she could afford to raise the children on her own. All she had to do was cut Van from her life, and the lives of the children, completely. Dani had even offered new identities for them all so she wouldn't have to worry about Van coming after them to claim custody. That was how far she was prepared to go.

Kayla had thought things like that were to be found solely in soap operas and the movies, not in everyday people's lives. It seemed too impossible to contemplate. Besides, she'd already signed a contract with Van. She was still bound by that, wasn't she? She balled up the paper towel and cast it in the trash bin. Could she do that to him? Disappear without a trace? Wouldn't that be the utmost cruelty?

But what about the way he'd just excised himself from their lives when he'd taken that job overseas? she asked herself. Was that really the kind of father she wanted for her children? A man who would come and go at will without any consideration for them?

Kayla looked at her reflection in the mirror. She was pale but relatively composed. Dani would be waiting at the table and she needed to go back and face up to the other woman's offer. Even as she left the restroom and walked back to their table, she had no idea what to say. However, once she was settled back in her chair, Dani didn't waste any time on working to convince her to see things her way.

"All under control again now, are we?" she said with a saccharine smile.

"Yes, thank you."

"I couldn't go through what you're suffering, not to mention what else it's doing to your body." She gave an elegant shudder. "Far too messy and so undignified."

Kayla didn't say anything; she simply couldn't, because she knew if she opened her mouth, she'd say something she'd probably regret. She was beginning to see what Imelda had warned her of. Dani obviously had no maternal urge at all—no idea of the love a mother bore for her child, no matter what carrying that child did to her. Dignity didn't even begin to enter into the equation. But it also made her wonder what Dani felt she offered Van. Surely no woman that focused on composure could truly feel passion for anyone. She didn't love him—she seemed to want to acquire him instead.

"So, what do you think of my offer?" Dani continued. "It's more than generous, and with the additional college funds established for the children, you should have no concerns for their future, either. Like I said, I want Donovan back. We're good together, and since you've been back on the scene with your growing brood, he's been different. Unhappy. Unfocused. He needs me more than he knows, and with you and the children out of the way, he won't have the distractions that have derailed our plans for our business and for a future together."

Unhappy? Maybe he'd been unhappy recently, but certainly not all the time. Kayla thought for a moment of the laughter she'd heard when he'd been playing with Sienna out on the lawn the other day. He certainly hadn't sounded unhappy then. But then she remembered the expression on his face when he caught her watching them and what an outsider it had made her feel like. "He said he wants the children. It was his choice to be a part of their lives."

"Is that what he told you?" Dani shook her head sorrowfully. "Oh, you poor deluded girl. Of course Donovan would want you to believe that, because that would be the right thing to do. But trust me, deep down, he doesn't want children cluttering up his life. He would do whatever he had to to ensure they were taken care of, of course. But he never, ever, wanted to be involved in raising children himself.

"With all the pressure this situation has put on him, he's been distracted at work and I'm sure you will agree that such a thing in his line of business can be dangerous. It's my desire to rid him of said distractions so he can put his mind where it's most valuable."

"On business, or on you?" Kayla asked bitterly.

"Both, of course. We are one and the same, after all. Donovan and I are meant to be together, Kayla. Surely you can see that. We're similar in so many ways—we have the same dreams, the same purpose. We're perfect for one another and we always will be. I understand he has needs. He is, after all, such a lusty creature, as I'm sure you know." Dani trilled a little laugh that scraped along Kayla's nerve endings and made her bristle with anger.

"Why would I know that?" She kept her voice cool, desperate not to betray the emotions that burned just beneath the surface.

"Oh, you know what I'm talking about." Dani gave her a conspiratorial look. "Donovan and I don't keep secrets from one another."

He'd told her about sleeping with Kayla? How could he? More important, why would he? Unless it had meant absolutely nothing to him at all. Unless he'd merely done it to try to work an itch out of his system.

Kayla stared at the pen. Gold, of course, with some fancy name engraved on it. It probably cost more than her last car did. Could she do this? Could she sign the offer that Dani had presented her and simply vanish from Van's life with his children? She wondered about the legal ramifications of that, about whether or not he'd pursue her.

"Questions, Kayla?" Dani pushed into her thoughts.

"Van threatened me with legal action if he didn't have access to the children the last time. Who's to say he won't do that again if I agree to your terms?"

"Should such a thing happen, and I assure you it won't, I will take care of everything for you, I promise. Here, I'll even write that in." She took the contract back and wrote in an addendum on the last page, marking her initials beside it. Skimming over it, Kayla noticed that it transferred legal liability for any conflicts to Dani. "He'll listen to me," Dani assured her.

"And you're certain he doesn't want the children anymore? He fought me hard to have shared custody of them. You're absolutely sure he's changed his mind about that now?"

"Well, obviously." Dani looked quite pointedly at the new contract. "As I said, his sense of honor demanded he do something about his children even though he didn't want them."

"And his sense of honor has disappeared now? Why didn't he talk to me about this? Why leave it to you?"

"Let's just say that the reality of being a father has turned into something he didn't expect. And, let's be honest, it's all getting so untidy, isn't it? Far better I deal with it and present him with a lovely clean slate to move forward with."

Dani's words had a ring of truth to them, but could Kayla trust them—or even trust the woman herself? She looked at the contract and thought hard about it. She'd admitted to herself only yesterday that she wanted out of the situation she'd found herself in. And there was no way she'd leave Sienna behind if she did find a way to leave. Dani was offering her a way out for both of them. A very lucrative way. As much as she hated to admit it, the woman's offer was tempting.

Kayla's biggest concern all along had been that Van would bail on his new family when things became too much for him on an emotional level. And hadn't he already proved that to be true after the night they'd slept together? He'd shut down completely since, ensuring she understood she had no future with him, nothing at all. And here she had a gold-plated opportunity to get out and stay out. A chance to start her life over.

"He wouldn't need to know where I've gone, would he?" she asked.

Dani, obviously sensing she was getting closer to her goal, gave Kayla the most genuine smile Kayla had seen from her so far. "Not at all. I'll make sure that Donovan is completely unaware of the finer details of our agreement and I've promised to ensure you're protected from him legally. He won't bother you again, trust me—we'll be too busy building our future."

Everything in Kayla screamed at her not to do it. She *wanted* Van to bother her—she wanted him in her life and in the lives of their children. But did he want the same thing?

No, he did not.

She made her decision, all the while feeling as though she was watching from the outside of some kind of glass prison. Her fingers clasped around the ornate gold pen. She had to do this, didn't she? It was what was best for Sienna and for Kayla's unborn son—and, ultimately, no matter how much it hurt, it was what was best for her. Their little family of three would want for nothing under the terms of the agreement. They'd have their own place, not be in forced living conditions under the roof of a man who now barely tolerated her presence.

"This is costing you a lot of money," she hedged. "Are *you* certain you want to do this?"

Dani made a shooing motion with her hand. "It's nothing to me financially. Donovan, however, is everything to me and as I said earlier, I'll do whatever it takes to have him back and make him happy again."

The last four words she uttered echoed in Kayla's mind. Yes, she was doing this not just for herself and for the children; she was doing this for Van, too. He deserved to be happy, didn't he?

She picked up the pen and scored her signature on the page.

Fourteen

He'd irrationally looked forward to coming home for days now. Normally he had no difficulty staying away, doing his job, losing himself in the work, but this trip had felt different. He'd had plenty of time at night, when he couldn't sleep, to search his soul for why and it had come as a painful revelation to admit to himself that he missed Kayla and Sienna with an ache that went soul deep.

Initially he'd dismissed it—putting it down to the fact that he was on the East Coast, a long way from the life he'd carved out for himself, and the fact that he was averaging sixteen- to eighteen-hour days and less than four hours' sleep each night. It was hard on a body and sleep deprivation could do awful things to a man's mind. He knew that intimately from his time in the army.

It only made sense that he'd crave an alternate existence, he'd reasoned, especially when that alternative lived so enticingly under his very roof. But, he'd reminded himself often, even that wouldn't last. As soon as his son was born and weaned, Kayla would be gone again and they'd share custody of the two children. Live sensible, detached parallel lives just the way he'd dictated all along. The way he wanted it, he reminded himself.

Somehow, though, he didn't want to live like that anymore. Somewhere along the line he'd felt a shift in his thinking—sensible and detached wasn't nearly enough now. And he couldn't use the argument that Kayla was unreliable—she was not the flighty dreamer she'd been in her younger years. Yes, she still had an impulsive and giving heart and always wanted to help those in worse circumstances than her own— to her detriment, as he'd seen—but that in itself didn't make her a bad person. She was a really good, loving and consistent mom, and considering the toll her pregnancies had taken on her physically, he had to admire that she hadn't let her physical complications deter her from her vow to her sister. That took guts no matter which way you looked at it.

"You need to man up," he said out loud, thumping the steering wheel beneath his hands. "Be honest with yourself."

And maybe, like Kayla had said, stop running scared from his emotions. But could he learn to trust like she wanted him to? Could he open himself up to his fears of inadequacy, rejection and failure? First it had been the parents who'd brought him up who'd scarred his heart. Then it had been the truth about his birth family that had put the seal on it. And he was damaged goods, let's face it. With a predisposition to alcoholism and a past in which he'd done unspeakable things to unspeakable people in the line of duty, he was no prize. And yet she said she loved him.

Would she love him as much if she knew all of it? Was it too late to make amends? Could he mend the rift he'd created when he'd shoved her love away as if it didn't matter—as if *she* didn't matter?

But she mattered, as did Sienna and his as-yet-unborn son. They mattered far more than he'd ever believed possible. He had to make things right—there really was no other option. His life would be incomplete if he couldn't fix things and create the true home he'd always wished for. Van slowed down for the turn into his driveway and waited for the electronic gates to slide open. Now that he was here, he was filled with an equal mix of foreboding and anticipation. It wouldn't be easy asking for Kayla's forgiveness, but he was prepared to humble his pride, go on his knees and beg if it meant she'd give him another chance. And this time, please, God, he wouldn't mess it up.

Van could sense something was wrong the minute he pulled into the garage. He looked around. Kayla's car was there, baby seat secured in the back, just like it always was—and yet he still felt as though something was terribly out of kilter.

He couldn't dismiss the feeling. His instincts had saved him from bad situations more times than he could count—both as a kid and as an adult. He hefted his laptop case from his car and went inside. There, his unease grew and it wasn't until he bumped into Imelda, who was coming down the hall toward him, that he realized something had to be very wrong. There was a sadness about her, an emptiness in her eyes that struck fear deep into his chest.

"Imelda? What is it? What's wrong?" he demanded.

"You don't know?"

"Know what? Tell me." Van fought the urge to shake it from her. "Is Kayla all right? The babies?"

"As far as I know, they're all very well. Perhaps I should let Ms. Matthews tell you. She's waiting for you out on the balcony."

"As far as you... Dani?"

But Imelda pushed past him with a sniff that sounded suspiciously like she was holding back tears. Without wasting another moment, Van strode through the house and headed outside. Dani lounged on one of the outdoor chairs, looking as exquisitely beautiful as always but so cold and emotionless that as he watched her unfold from her seat and rise to greet him, he wondered how he could ever have thought he'd be happy with someone like her.

"Donovan, darling," Dani greeted him, presenting a cheek to be kissed. "I've missed you."

Van couldn't bring himself to touch her. Not now.

"I'm surprised to see you here," he said through gritted teeth, forcing himself to be civil when all he wanted to do was demand she tell him where Kayla was and why she wasn't here. "I wasn't expecting to see you until tomorrow at the office."

"I know—isn't it delicious? I love my little surprises." She turned to the table and lifted a bottle of champagne from the sweating ice bucket in the center of the table. "Now you're back, this calls for a celebration."

"Dani, what the hell is going on?" he growled.

"Oh, no need to go all caveman on me, Donovan. You know that doesn't appeal to me. Besides, you're going to be so pleased when you know what I've done."

She passed him a crystal champagne flute, which he promptly put back on the table. "You know I don't drink," he bit out.

"But this is a very special occasion. Surely you can make an exception, just this once? Just a sip?"

"I don't make exceptions. Not on this, ever. Why are you here?"

"I thought you might be pleased to know I've managed to sort out your little situation and get rid of it permanently so we can go back to how we were before. You've been so wretched since you've had that woman and her brat under your roof. Someone had to do something."

"That's my child you're referring to," he said, pressing down the fury that threatened to boil over. His anger would have to wait until he got all the information he needed, and if he knew Dani at all, that was probably going to take a lot longer than he wanted.

"One you didn't want, remember. And now she's gone. And her mother, too."

"What did you do to them?"

"Do? Why, nothing. I merely offered them an alternative and now the situation is resolved to everyone's satisfaction. We can go back to our plans to marry without any unwanted babies cluttering up our future."

Was he going to have to drag everything out of her word by painful word? "Where are they?"

"They're quite happy where they are. At Kayla's request, you're not to know the exact location. We both felt it would be better that way. Otherwise, given your unfortunate knight-in-shining-armor tendencies, you'd be inclined to haring after her, wouldn't you?"

"You had no right to interfere. We're over as a couple, Dani. Our relationship remains a business one only."

She fluttered an elegant hand and he noted the solitaire diamond ring he'd given her glittered once more on her ring finger. "But we both know we want more than that. We were happy before she came along."

Happy? He might have thought he'd been happy but he hadn't realized quite how empty his life had been.

"Dani, I made a mistake when I asked you to marry me. It wasn't fair to either of us."

For the first time, her confidence wavered a bit. Apparently this was not what she'd expected him to say. "What are you saying, Donovan? Please, think very hard before you answer me. We have so much riding on this. Our business, our future, everything."

Was she insinuating that their business would always come first? Hell, what was he thinking? Of course it did. It was what had brought them together, after all. He'd been an idiot to think that would ever have been enough to build a marriage on.

"You deserve better than me, Dani," he said firmly. "You deserve a man who will love you through and through—everyone does. We might have been happy together, initially, at least, but long-term I think we both know we would have been left wanting more."

"But I want you, Donovan."

She said the words flatly, as if wanting was all that was important.

"I'm not the man you think I am anymore. Maybe I never was. I'm sorry, but it really is over between us."

A look of regret flashed through her eyes. "And the business? Do you still expect me to work beside you knowing you've rejected me like this?" She hadn't objected before…but she must have thought the situation between them could still be resolved. Kayla had been wrong about Dani—she'd fought for him after all. But not out of love, simply out of pride. Dani hadn't wanted to lose out on the relationship she'd decided would suit her best. And now that he'd injured that pride by clearly rejecting her, she evidently wanted nothing more to do with him.

He sighed. It would probably take every penny he had, and maybe the house, as well, but he could buy her out. He'd miss her business acumen, but he realized that a man needed more than that by his side and in his bed.

It was probably a testament to how little her heart was invested in their relationship that they managed to hammer out a verbal agreement there and then regarding the transfer of her company shares. Their lawyers would get rich taking care of the rest.

"I'm sorry it had to come to this," Dani said as she rose from the table.

"So am I," he said, taking her hand and clasping it warmly. For a long time he'd thought she'd be the woman he'd spend the rest of his life with. She had his respect at the very least. But there was one question still burning in the back of his mind. "You know where Kayla is, don't you?"

"I do, but Donovan, I won't tell you where to find her. Trust me on this. You may think you know what you want but I think in this instance I know you better. She's no good for you. She's moved away of her own choice. Yes, I helped her, of course I did. She had no one else, did she? Let's face it—you have never really been there since she moved in with you, have you? Your work has always been the most important thing to you and that's why we were so good together." Tears gleamed in Dani's eyes. "But remember this—she could have told me no. She could have stayed, and she didn't."

"I have a responsibility to see to it that my children are going to be okay." That was only a fraction of the reason, but he thought it was the one most likely to get a positive response from Dani. She wouldn't like hearing that Kayla had won his heart when Dani hadn't even made a dent in it.

"Already seen to," Dani said with a slight wobble in her voice. "Think of it as my parting gift to you. I set up generous funds for them and an excellent housing situation. They're fine, and Kayla, well, she'd be happier if she never saw you again, too."

Would she? He'd find that out for himself, he decided as he showed Dani to the door and called for Jacob to organize someone to take her to the airport and for a pilot to fly her back to San Francisco. The moment she left the house, he was on the phone to his immediate team with instructions.

"Find her and soon," he directed. "This takes priority over everything else right now."

The apartment just outside Sacramento held everything she needed, Kayla thought, and was far nicer than the one she'd been living in before she'd moved to Van's. Sienna had adjusted easily to the move and aside from the occasional tantrum when she would utter "Dadadadad!" in imperious tones as only a thirteen-month-old could do, she didn't seem to miss Van, either. But Kayla did. With an ache that went deep into her very being and that kept her awake nights and tearful at the least opportune times. Just hormones, she told herself. Life would settle into a new pattern soon and she'd adjust, like she always did.

The baby's movements had become more frequent and stronger of late. As if Van's little boy was trying to make a statement of his own. Maybe he was simply expressing his approval of the move. She wondered what Van had felt when he'd arrived home and found she and Sienna were gone. Relief, probably. While he definitely had a strong urge to control and protect, there was an emptiness in him where his heart should have been. She felt sorry for him, truly sorry, but at the same time she felt sorry for herself, too.

Sienna was curled up in bed after a busy day. They'd joined a local playgroup and Kayla was tentatively making new friendships. The fact that the babies' father wasn't on the scene hadn't been easy to gloss over and the sympathy reflected in a couple of the other moms' eyes had almost been her undoing but she'd held it together. The gentle offers of help and support from her new friends had been welcome and made her feel just a little less alone than she had when she arrived.

She was just settling down with a cup of lemon ginger tea, and trying not to think about Van, when there was a buzz from downstairs. She checked the security screen to see who was at her door. Van? A visceral shudder ran through her body—even the grainy black-and-white image on the screen did nothing to reduce the impact seeing him again had on her. No, a thousand times, no! How had he found her? Dani had told her that her location here would be a complete secret.

But then again, Kayla hadn't factored in what Van did for a living. Part of providing security was gathering intelligence. She should have thought about that further. Clearly changing her name hadn't been enough. She should have moved across the country, as well. Either way, it was too late now.

The buzzing became insistent.

"Go away," she said through the intercom.

"I need to see you, Kayla. Let me into the building."

"Look, I made my decision and I'm sticking with it. Please, Van, respect me on this if nothing else," she begged.

"I'm not leaving until we've talked. Now, I can spend all night leaning on this buzzer, and the buzzers for all your neighbors, or you can let me in and we can talk."

"I'll call the police," she threatened, knowing in her heart of hearts she would do no such thing.

"And explain to them that you have abducted my daughter? Please, by all means, go ahead. I'll be more than happy to show them the court-issued document I have in my pocket awarding me full custody of Sienna."

"You've come to take her away? You can't do that!"

Through the crackle of the speaker, she heard him sigh. "No, Kayla, that's not what I'm here for, but I'm not above using this document to get to you if that's what it takes."

There was a determination in his tone that left her in no doubt that he'd do exactly as he'd said.

"All you want to do is talk?"

She couldn't hide the tremor in her voice as she spoke and gripped her hands into fists of frustration beside her. How would she ever maintain the upper hand in a discussion with him if she couldn't even talk to him through a speaker without getting overemotional?

"For now," he replied. She could hear his impatience.

"And then you'll be on your way?"

"For now," he repeated.

She hit the button that unlocked the downstairs door and said, "Apartment 303."

"I know."

He probably knew everything by now. In some ways the thought was a relief, but in others? Well, she'd cross those bridges when she got to them, just like she always did. She opened her front door and waited for the chime of the elevator down the hall. She didn't have to wait long.

If she'd thought her gut response to Van's image on the screen had been strong, it was nothing compared to how she felt as he strode out of the elevator and down the corridor toward her. As dark and saturnine as ever and dressed in a black fitted T-shirt and black jeans, he looked as if he was on a stealth mission. A frisson of fear rippled across the back of her neck and she stepped away the moment he drew near.

Van's eyes scanned her thoroughly and she felt their intensity as if it was a physical touch. Her body responded in kind, her nipples beading into tight points, a flare of desire burning at her core.

"Come in. Make yourself at home," she said pithily as he stepped inside. "Just close the door behind you."

He did exactly that and she stood in the middle of the room, watching him as he made himself quite comfortable on her sofa and stretched his legs out before him. He looked as if he was here for no more than a social visit, but she knew the truth.

"How did you find me? Did Dani—?"

"She didn't tell me a word and she was better at

hiding you than I thought she'd be. Did you know she set up a corporation to rent this place for you and to administer the money for your upkeep?"

Kayla nodded. She, too, had been surprised at the lengths Dani had been prepared to go to hide her trail, but she'd been so glad for an out that she hadn't stopped to think about the how—she'd just wanted to be gone.

"Why, Kayla? Why leave me? I thought that was my specialty," he said ruefully.

His attempt at humor fell dreadfully flat, at least as far as she was concerned.

"I had to do what was best for the children," she said vehemently. At least, that was what she'd constantly told herself as she lay in bed at night, reliving their lovemaking and wishing she could convince herself it was better to be away and trying to be happy than to be with him and miserable instead.

"How is Sienna doing?"

Kayla nodded. "She's fine. Adjusting happily and making friends at playgroup."

"They make friends at this age?"

"Well, they play alongside one another," she conceded.

"Good. I'm glad she's okay. And the baby? Have you been to the doctor? I'm assuming you transferred to a new doctor up here?"

She nodded. "Everything is textbook perfect. Look, Van, stop beating around the bush. Sienna's fine, the baby's fine and I'm fine. What do you want?"

"I want you back."

"That's not going to happen. We tried it—it didn't work. In my newfound maturity I'm trying to learn from my mistakes. Besides, Dani told me that the two of you were together again, that you wanted me gone."

Finally a slow-burning anger began to take over the anxiety. She fed on it, allowed it to grow and take shape, knowing she'd need it to buoy her through the next few minutes.

"Look, Van, we're happy here without you. We don't need you. We never did, to be honest." She crossed her fingers behind her back. "My children deserve stability and constancy in their lives. And we both know you're incapable of that. I know you can shower them with everything that money can buy and send them to the best schools, but I also know that you won't be there for them when they really need you, because you won't let yourself love them—or anyone else."

Van looked at her, pain reflected in his eyes. She felt a pang of remorse for being so blunt but someone had to say it. The time for tiptoeing around the truth was long past.

"That might have been true of me before, but it's not true now. And as to Dani—she's in my past, where she belongs. She might have hoped we'd get back together, but that's never going to happen. We no longer even work together. She should never have interfered. I mean it when I say I want you back home, Kayla. You and Sienna."

Kayla sighed and shook her head as she sat in one of the armchairs opposite the sofa. "Van, you say you want us there now, but how can you be sure? You can't just turn love on and off like a tap—there when it's convenient for you and gone when it's not."

"You're right, but I can learn if you'll let me."

"And if you decide it's not for you after all? What then? You just make yourself emotionally and physically unavailable to your son and daughter and carry on with your life with a clear conscience, telling yourself you *tried*? That's not good enough. They deserve better than that. *I* deserve better than that."

And there it was. The crux of her pain, the center of everything. As much as she loved him, he just couldn't be the man she needed, and she'd rather have no one than suffer a life with a man who had a yawning cavern where his heart should be.

"I won't. I want to make a commitment to them, to you all, that I'll always be there for you. Being with you, well…" he shook his head "…it opened my eyes, made me see things I didn't want to see. Reminded me of things I always wanted but convinced myself I could do without—things I didn't deserve to have. For the first time since I was a kid and you and your sister lived next door, I started to feel like I belonged somewhere, to someone."

"None of that guarantees me anything," she retorted. "I don't want to live with the fear that one day I'll wake up again and reach for you and you'll be gone. And what if, next time, you don't come back? How on earth am I supposed to deal with that? More important, how are the children?"

"It won't happen," he insisted.

"But how do I know that?"

"Because I'm stepping back from operations, for good. The company is undergoing some restructuring and the operations division is going to be under the control of a team I trust implicitly. A team on which I am only to be an adviser rather than an on-site operator. I've always prided myself on the fact that I wouldn't send my people into the field unless I was prepared to go there myself—it's who I've always been. But I learned that I've changed. I have a responsibility to the ones I love, to be there for them. I don't want to put myself in a position where I might die and leave you behind, Kayla."

Kayla looked at him in disbelief. "You really expect me to believe that?"

"I wish you would. The same as I wish you would give me a last chance to show you I can be the man you need, the father the children need. I've learned a lot these past few weeks, not least of which is that emotion is not always a weakness. It can be a strength, too. I've always been too afraid to feel, because when I did, it only hurt or led to being a weapon that allowed others to hurt me. It was easier to simply stop caring."

Her eyes filled with tears and they began to spill down her cheeks unhindered. "Van, I'm so sorry."

"Don't be sorry for me, Kayla. Just tell me that you love me. Just tell me…" His voice broke and he dragged in a breath before continuing. "Just tell me, please, that you'll let me love you, too."

"I want to, Van, I really do, but I don't know if I

can trust you. And it's not just me I'm talking about, but Sienna and this little guy here, too." She rubbed her small round belly protectively. "I can't let you into our lives again if you're only going to walk out when the going gets tough."

"I don't want to be that man anymore. I want to feel. I want to experience love and enjoy my life and I know I won't be able to do that without you by my side. I don't know why I never saw it before, why I kept pushing it away. I want to go to sleep at night and know that the first ray of sunshine in my life each morning will be seeing you there by my side. I know I've treated you badly but I can't let you go. I never understood why, Kayla, but it's because I love you—even when I didn't want to, I loved you. I just didn't know how to deal with it."

She wiped her face dry. He was saying all the right things but did he believe them himself? Could she? "What makes you think you can deal with it now?"

"That's a good question. I think I've finally realized what's important in life. I've spent all my years trying to find myself worthy in one way or another. When I didn't find that at home, with my adoptive parents, I looked for it in the army. And I was a damn good soldier. I fit there. I could hone my instincts and my skills and be great at something and be proud that what I was doing was serving the greater good. But I still never found that elusive sense of home that I was searching for. When I quit the army, I knew I had the skills to make a lot of money, so I did. I carved a new niche for myself, created a place where I thought I'd made a home. But it wasn't a home until you lived there, too. Having you and Sienna under my roof reminded me of what it felt like being at your parents' house. Feeling the love your family shared for one another. Even when your parents were angry at you, you could still feel that they loved you. It was something that was constant and I wanted that constancy but I didn't feel like I'd ever earned it. And when you offered it, I didn't know how to handle it."

Kayla stared at him. She'd never seen him look this shattered or broken inside. Not even when Sienna died, or on that awful morning years ago when she and her sister had found him curled up asleep on their front porch with bruises from head to foot courtesy of his dad.

"Van, you don't *earn* love. It's not a reward for good behavior. It's something freely given," she said softly.

"I'm learning that now," he said with an ironic quirk of his lips. "Your family was the only thing that kept me from running away as a kid. Did you know that?"

Kayla nodded. Her sister had told her one night after they'd heard yelling from Van's house that she wished Van would just run away because then he might get put into foster care and surely that would be better than what he endured in his own home. But he stayed, until he was eighteen.

"What made you join the army?" she asked. "You could have gone away to college, gone anywhere. But you enlisted."

"I had a lot of anger in me. I needed to channel it somewhere with a purpose or I knew I'd go off the rails. I'd started drinking already, using a fake ID or stealing my dad's beers from the fridge. It was a problem before I even knew it. And that's something else you need to know, Kayla. I'm an alcoholic. There, I've said it. That's the first time I've admitted it to myself—did you know that? I'm an alcoholic and I come from a long line of alcoholics. The reason I was put up for adoption was because my birth parents had fallen so deep into substance abuse that they could no longer care for me. And the scary thing is, their DNA is in me, and in our children."

He dropped his head and stared at the floor, Kayla battled the desire to go to him and comfort him. She was beginning to understand a whole lot more about Van Murphy and the way he'd behaved. Both his self-destructive behaviors and the ones that were the exact opposite, when he found it necessary to control and protect everything around him.

"DNA is one thing, but you still make your own choices, Van."

He coughed a humorless laugh. "Yeah, I read somewhere that DNA loads the gun and environment pulls the trigger. Well, I kept pushing myself into environments that made me very dangerous. It got to the point where I chased death. You know, when I agreed to be a donor for your sister, I never believed I'd live long enough to see her bear her children. It was only after she died that I realized that I didn't want to stay on that fast road to a short future." He sat up and looked Kayla straight in the eye. "The first time we made love was the first time I felt truly alive, but it terrified me so much more than anything I'd ever done before. That's why I left you. I didn't know how to deal with how you made me feel or how much I wanted to stay with you. I felt like I had to punish myself for wanting to be with you. Like I'd failed you somehow, or disrespected you. I had to punish myself for that, so I had to leave. In the end, I decided to blame the whole episode on the drink, y'know? And I stopped drinking from that night on to make sure I wouldn't make the same mistake again.

"Not long after that, I discovered the truth about my birth parents and everything slotted into place about who and what I was. I was glad I'd left you then. I wasn't worthy of love or family. I was glad that my parents' problem ended with me. That was my choice, my decision. And with your sister gone, God rest her beautiful soul, I wouldn't have kids, ever."

The last pieces fell into place and painful understanding dawned. "Until I turned up in your office with one and wanting to have more of them. I'm so sorry, Van. I had no idea."

"I've tried to be strong. I've worked hard to make the right choices. But deep down, I'm still a weak man. I have no idea how to be a good father, Kayla. With my background of violence and alcohol and the very fact it's ingrained into me, how could I be?"

Her heart fractured on his words. Despite what she'd kept telling herself, she could see he had a heart. One that was broken and bruised and buried deep beneath so many years of abuse that it was a fragile thing. One that needed constancy and tenderness to thrive. She could do that—she could help his love thrive and grow. And together they could give their children the love, devotion and stability they needed to teach them what was right and wrong and guide them through their lives. They would give their all to them and hope that it would be enough.

"All it takes is love, Van. Just love. Together we can do this, I promise."

"Together?"

The look in his eyes, the yearning and hope she saw there, shrank all her fears into a tiny knot in the recesses of her heart. Maybe someday the knot would go away, and maybe it wouldn't, but she knew if it didn't, she'd learn to manage it because Van deserved for her to try. When had he ever known unconditional love? When had he ever been told he deserved it just as much as anyone else? Someone had to show him and that started with her.

"Yes, together," she said firmly. She got up from her chair and dropped to her knees in front of him. "I love you, Van Murphy. You don't need to be alone anymore, ever, but promise me you won't push me away when you most need me. Promise me you'll let me love you the way you deserve to be loved."

"I do promise. I know I'm not worthy of you," he said. "But I want you so much I don't feel like a whole person unless you're with me. Does that make me weak, Kayla?"

His honesty drove right through her. "No," she assured him. "Admitting it is what makes you strong. Fear is what makes us brave in the long run. Doing what's right, even when we're scared. That's what makes the difference. And, Van, loving you is what's right for me. We'll make it through this."

Van reached for her and pulled her to him. "You know, I believe you. I love you so much, Kayla. Please, don't ever leave me again."

She smiled up at him. "Only if you promise the same."

"I do," he said fervently. "I really do. Will you come home with me tomorrow? You and Sienna? Will you be my family?"

"We already are," she answered.

Kayla lifted her face to his and as his lips claimed hers in a seal of their declaration to one another, she knew they'd weather the storms that would undoubtedly come their way.

Together.

Always.

* * * * *

*If you liked this story of a billionaire tamed
by the love of the right woman—and her baby—
pick up these other novels from
USA TODAY bestselling author
Yvonne Lindsay
A FATHER'S SECRET
THE CHILD THEY DIDN'T EXPECT
WANTING WHAT SHE CAN'T HAVE
FOR THE SAKE OF THE SECRET CHILD*

Available now from Harlequin Desire!

*And don't miss the next
BILLIONAIRES AND BABIES story,
THE BABY PROPOSAL
by Andrea Laurence
Available December 2016!*

*If you're on Twitter, tell us what you think of
Harlequin Desire! #harlequindesire*

COMING NEXT MONTH FROM

HARLEQUIN *Desire*

Available December 6, 2016

#2485 THE BABY PROPOSAL
Billionaires and Babies • by Andrea Laurence
Lana will do anything to gain custody of her infant niece—even marry her best friend, Kal, in name only. But playing house in Kal's mansion has them both wanting to be much more than friends...

#2486 THE TEXAN'S ONE-NIGHT STANDOFF
Dynasties: The Newports • by Charlene Sands
Brooks Newport's scorching one-night stand with Ruby Lopez was unforgettable—and he wants more! Until a reunion with his long-lost father reveals Ruby to be an honorary member of the family...and completely off-limits.

#2487 MAID UNDER THE MISTLETOE
by Maureen Child
After a tragic past, millionaire Sam Henry enjoys being alone, especially for Christmas. But will his temporary holiday housekeeper's sexy smiles and enticing touch lure him back into the world—and tempt him to take a second chance on love?

#2488 THE PREGNANCY PROJECT
Love and Lipstick • by Kat Cantrell
Dante has made a fortune as Dr. Sexy. So he knows attraction when he feels it—even when the temptation is his pregnant best friend who's sworn off men! Now this expert at seduction must prove his theories work—while holding on to his heart.

#2489 RICH RANCHER FOR CHRISTMAS
The Beaumont Heirs • by Sarah M. Anderson
CJ Wesley is a Beaumont heir, and that's a secret he won't share. Especially not with a sexy-as-sin city girl looking for her next big story. But when a snowstorm strands these opposites on his ranch, their white-hot attraction proves impossible to resist!

#2490 MARRIED TO THE MAVERICK MILLIONAIRE
From Mavericks to Married • by Joss Wood
Millionaire hockey star Quinn agrees to a marriage of convenience to avoid scandal and save the biggest deal of his career. But an unplanned kiss at a masked ball ignites a fiery attraction to his new wife he can't ignore...

HDCNM1116

*Lana will do anything to gain custody of her infant
niece—even marry her best friend, Kal, in name only.
But playing house in Kal's mansion has them both
wanting to be much more than friends...*

*Read on for a sneak peek at
THE BABY PROPOSAL,
Andrea Laurence's latest in the bestselling
BILLIONAIRES AND BABIES series!*

"What about moving in with me?"

Lana looked at him, narrowing her eyes. "That would
help a lot, actually. Are you sure, though? It's going to be
a major cramp on your bachelorhood to have me and a
baby in the house."

Kal shrugged that off. He rarely had time for anything
aside from work this time of year. Plus, if Lana was in the
house with the baby, he wouldn't miss out on his time with
her. He'd never admit to his selfish motivations, however.
"I've got three extra bedrooms just sitting empty. If it will
help, I'm happy to do what I can."

Lana beamed at him. "I'm actually really glad you
said that, because I was just about to get to the crazy part
of my plan."

Kal swallowed hard. She had something in mind that
was crazier than moving in together with a baby?

Just then Lana slid off her chair and onto one knee in

front of him. She took his hand and held it as he frowned down at her. "What are you doing?" he asked as his chest grew tight and he struggled to breathe. His hand was suddenly burning up where she held it in hers, the contact lighting his every nerve on fire. He wanted to pull away and regain control of himself, but he knew he couldn't. This was just the calm before the storm.

Lana took a deep breath and looked up at him with a hopeful smile. "I'm asking you to marry me."

Don't miss
THE BABY PROPOSAL
by Andrea Laurence,
available December 2016 wherever
Harlequin® Desire books and ebooks are sold.

www.Harlequin.com

Whatever You're Into… Passionate Reads

Looking for more passionate reads from Harlequin®?
Fear not! Harlequin® Presents, Harlequin® Desire and
Harlequin® Blaze offer you irresistible romance stories
featuring powerful heroes.

❖HARLEQUIN® *Presents*®

Do you want alpha males, decadent glamour and jet-set
lifestyles? Step into the sensational, sophisticated world of
Harlequin® Presents, where sinfully tempting heroes ignite a
fierce and wickedly irresistible passion!

❖HARLEQUIN® *Desire*

Harlequin® Desire novels are powerful, passionate and
provocative contemporary romances set against a backdrop of
wealth, privilege and sweeping family saga. Alpha heroes with
a soft side meet strong-willed but vulnerable heroines amid a
dramatic world of divided loyalties, high-stakes conflict and
intense emotion.

❖HARLEQUIN® *Blaze*

Harlequin® Blaze stories sizzle with strong heroines and
irresistible heroes playing the game of modern love and lust.
They're fun, sexy and always steamy.

Be sure to check out our full selection of books
within each series every month!

www.Harlequin.com